The Emergency Zoo

Miriam Halahmy

ALMA BOOKS LTD
3 Castle Yard
Richmond
Surrey TW10 6TF
United Kingdom
www.almabooks.com

First published by Alma Books Ltd in 2016

Printed and bound by CPI Group (UK) Ltd, Croydon, CR0 4YY

ISBN: 978-1-84688-397-2

The Emergency Zoo

FOR JACOB

WITH LOVE

If you and your family have to leave home at very short notice, on no account leave your animals in the house or turn them into the street.

If you cannot place them in the care of neighbours, it really is kindest to have them destroyed.

extract from 'Advice to Animal Owners',
Ministry of Home Security, 25th August 1939

At the going down of the sun and in the morning,
We will remember them.

from 'For the Fallen' by
Robert Laurence Binyon

Chapter 1

THE DEN

Saturday 26th August 1939

"Hi there!" called Tilly.

Rosy waved back from the bridge over the canal.

"Come on, Bonny." Tilly turned her bike onto the towpath, her little dog trotting behind.

Rosy was leaning over her bike basket, tucking a piece of pink flannel around her cat.

"How's Tinkerbell this morning?" asked Tilly as she pedalled onto the bridge.

"Fine and dandy," said Rosy, stroking along Tinkerbell's golden back.

"Come on then, let's go!"

Bonny gave a high-pitched bark and ran forward as Tilly pushed off and whizzed down the slope onto the opposite bank.

"Wait for me," called out Rosy, setting off at a wobble.

They had to slow down anyway as they rode onto wasteland between the deserted factories. The ground was littered with broken glass and bits of metal which might puncture their tyres.

But very soon they reached a gap in a broken-down wall, and then fields opened up. Tilly set off at a fast pace over the bumpy ground towards a wood in the distance, Rosy's short legs struggling to keep up behind.

It only took a couple of minutes to reach the far end of the field. Then they had to push through brambles which tore at their skirts and scratched their bare arms, while Bonny tunnelled through the undergrowth. Finally they were in the clearing – Tilly let out a great whoop of joy and dropped her bike on the grass.

In front of them stood an old hut about the size of two big garden sheds put together. It had crumbling walls, there were holes in the roof and the door was half off, but it was their very own secret den. They'd discovered it at the beginning of the holidays, and had played there every day since.

Rosy lifted Tinkerbell out of her basket and propped her bike against a tree. "You change the water in the jam jars," she said. "I'll pick some fresh flowers."

"Then we could sweep the floor so everything's nice and tidy before lunch," called Tilly over her shoulder, as she and Bonny raced into the den.

Rosy wandered off, stroking Tinkerbell and looking around for flowers.

"Poppies near the field, daisies in the grass," she murmured, "a couple of yellow irises and there's a big foxglove under the oak tree."

Tilly couldn't help smiling to herself as she dumped the old flowers in the clearing and emptied out the stale water. Rosy knew the names of all the flowers and all the trees and pretty much anything else. It was as though she swallowed books whole. On her bookshelf in her bedroom, she had the ten volumes of Arthur Mee's encyclopaedia, which she carefully consulted whenever Tilly wanted to know anything, as well as more books than anyone else Tilly knew. Now that they were twelve and in the High School, Tilly needed Rosy's books more than ever for the masses of homework.

That's what's so wonderful about the holidays, Tilly thought, stretching her long frame. No homework for six whole weeks.

"Come on, Bonny," she called out, "let's go down to the stream." Bonny gave a delighted yap and raced off into the wood.

The stream had almost dried up in the summer, but then the weather broke with terrible thunderstorms, so the water was running freely again between mossy banks.

Bonny arrived first and splashed straight into the middle, lapping up the cool, fresh water. Pond skaters, with their tiny bodies and long spidery legs, skated across the surface of a pool trapped between tree roots. A cheery blackbird was singing above them, almost drowning out the sound of Bonny lapping away furiously.

Tilly slipped off her sandals and socks, tucked her dress into her knickers and paddled in after Bonny. The bed of the stream was muddy and Tilly liked the squishy feeling between her toes. Rosy was scared that creatures might be hiding in the mud and bite her, so she would only sit on the bank and dangle her feet in the water.

Once Tilly had filled the jam jars with fresh water, she climbed out of the stream, tucked her shoes and socks under her arm, and, whistling to Bonny, went back to the clearing, barefoot.

"Mind," warned Rosy, as she stood at the door of the den, a broken broom in her hand. "There's still nails around."

Over the summer they'd turned the den into their own little home, spending days tidying and organizing. Tilly thought the old hut probably belonged to a farmer, but the place was so full of cobwebs it was obvious no one came there any more. They'd bashed down the worst cobwebs on the walls and laid a couple of sacks like rugs on the earth floor. There were a few wooden crates and they'd set these out as seats. With fresh jars of flowers and an old bit of red velvet Tilly had begged from Mum, they'd made their very own cosy den.

"We're so lucky no one else has found out yet," she said now, as she took packets of sandwiches from the bike baskets.

"That's because we know how to keep a secret," said Rosy, sitting with her legs curled under her and Tinkerbell in her arms. The cat was licking her front paws with long, slow strokes as Rosy fondled an ear. "I do love the way cats' ears go up in points like elves," she said.

"Or Martians," said Tilly with a grin, as she flopped down in the long grass and pulled Bonny on her lap. "Our pets love the secret den as much we do," she said, kissing the large white patch on Bonny's forehead.

Bonny was a King Charles spaniel, nearly two years old. Her fur was a mixture of black, white and gold; she had long curly ears and huge brown eyes, which could melt the hardest heart.

Rosy was holding out a whole sardine to Tinkerbell. A deep purring was coming from the cat as she delicately nosed the fish.

"Where did you get that?" said Tilly.

"Pinched it from the larder without Megan noticing," said Rosy with a mischievous grin.

Tilly laughed and Tinkerbell opened her mouth and began taking small pieces of the sardine between her teeth. "She eats so much more politely than Bonny."

"Course," said Rosy, "cats don't wolf food because they're tigers really – don't you think Tinkerbell looks like a small tiger?" She stroked the tabby cat's golden fur with its black stripes.

"Terrifyingly so," mumbled Tilly through a mouthful of cheese and pickle sandwich.

The girls sat eating in the warm sunshine and Tilly fed Bonny some dog biscuits. Then they lay down on their fronts to read their books.

They lost all track of time, as usual, until Rosy said, "We have to go in twenty-five minutes or we'll be late for tea again."

"All right," said Tilly with a sigh. She took her book over to her bicycle, calling Bonny to follow.

"It's Sunday school in the morning, and then Megan's invited the vicar and his wife for lunch," said Rosy.

The girls rolled their eyes at each other.

"Poor you," said Tilly.

The vicar had a strange, high-pitched voice, and Tilly was always getting into trouble in Sunday school for dissolving into fits of giggles.

"He says I'm incorrigible," she muttered.

"Oh yes," said Rosy. "Incorrigible: not able to be corrected or reformed."

"Crikey, Rose, how on earth do you remember all that?"

"Sometimes I just read the dictionary – you know, for fun."

Rosy bent down to kiss Tinkerbell's button nose and the cat yawned and stretched herself.

"I need some fun right now," said Tilly, throwing herself to her feet. "I'm going to get to the top branch of the oak tree."

"Well hurry up, we have to go very soon." Rosy picked up Tinkerbell and took her into the den, where she could let her run free and explore without getting lost.

Tilly climbed into the lower branches of the tree and considered once more the branch above her head, which she hadn't quite reached all summer.

Today has to be the day, she told herself. Mum keeps saying I've grown out of everything, so I must be taller than I was at the end of term. She gave one huge push upwards on her long legs, stretching her fingers until she thought they'd come out of their sockets. For the first time she could feel the branch above her head and, reaching with both hands, she pulled herself up.

"I've done it! I've done it!" she called out in triumph, her face red with the effort.

"Well done," Rosy called back from the den. "Now come down so we can get ready to go."

"Coming," and in a few seconds, Tilly swung down to the lowest branch and landed on the grass. Bonny jumped up to lick her hand with delight.

CHAPTER 1

Tilly was the tallest girl in her class and the fastest runner. Rosy was a rather small person, three whole inches shorter than Tilly, with curly shoulder-length hair and tiny feet. She was top of everything at school, but Tilly was the daring one. Rosy worried about even the smallest things.

Which isn't surprising really, Tilly often reminded herself. Rosy lived with her married sister, Megan, and Megan's husband, Donald, who was a butcher. Rosy had lost her parents three years earlier, when they both caught pneumonia one freezing cold January.

Tilly had long ago decided Rosy was the bravest person she knew. She'd been weepy for the first few months, and then she'd buried herself in her books and hardly talked about her Mum and Dad again. Megan, who was twenty-five, was more like a very strict, frumpy parent than a big sister. She insisted on rules which drove Rosy mad, such as changing into slippers the minute she was inside the front door, and wearing gloves to church. Fortunately, Donald, who was ten years older than Megan, was funny and jolly, and often slipped Rosy extra pocket money or sweets on the quiet.

"I know Megan's my sister," Rosy had told Tilly. "And I'm lucky to have her, as she does say rather often, but really I'm an only child, like you."

"We're not just best friends," Tilly had declared. "We're like sisters. I mean, we've known each other since babies and we have so much in common, like reading and our pets."

"Absolutely," Rosy had replied.

Now Bonny started to run off towards the wood again and Tilly chased after her, slipping on a lead for the last few minutes as they packed everything away and Rosy settled Tinkerbell in her basket. The little cat was looking sleepy after playing ball in the den.

"Come on," said Rosy in an anxious voice. "Megan will shout at me if I'm late like yesterday."

"At least we have the ride home," said Tilly with a sigh, as they pushed through the thicket. Then they jumped on their bikes and rode back to their streets in West London, beyond the canal and their beautiful den.

"See you after lunch tomorrow," said Tilly, as they parted at the corner.

"Two thirty sharp," called out Rosy, as she pedalled away.

Still another whole week of the holidays, thought Tilly as she rode slowly home, Bonny loping beside her, tongue lolling out of the side of her mouth.

Chapter 2

THE KINDEST THING

Sunday afternoon, 27th August 1939

"Let's take our pets down to the stream and play by the water," said Tilly.

"I'll bring Tinkerbell's tent with us," said Rosy, gathering together a large piece of material with long strings hanging down from a crate in the den.

"Good idea. Come on, Bonny!" With a sharp whistle, Tilly set off for the wood.

It was another beautiful day and the afternoon sun was hot in the clearing. The girls had swept out the old leaves which had fallen into the hut since Saturday, and pinned up some pictures Tilly had drawn in Sunday school. Sundays always made her restless with everyone expecting her to "sit down and do something quietly." Dad mostly worked in the garden or listened to the radio. But Tilly felt the muscles in her legs almost screaming out for a long bike ride or a good run by lunchtime.

Grown-ups are so lazy, she'd grumble to herself. Why on earth does anyone ever need to sit down and be quiet? It's a complete waste of time.

Now she was outdoors again, running through the woods with Bonny and her best friend, and no grown-ups to bother them until teatime.

At the stream, Rosy and Tilly stretched out the torn sheet which Rosy had begged from Megan, and tied up two corners to the trees. Then they let the sides drop down to create a nice enclosure for Tinkerbell.

"We don't want you to get lost in the wood, do we?" said Rosy, crawling into the makeshift tent and dropping a ball of wool.

Tilly crawled in beside her, leaving Bonny to drink from the stream.

"Here, Tinks, catch," called Tilly as she grabbed the ball and threw it up in the air.

The girls giggled as Tinkerbell sat up, her head cocked on one side, ears pricked, watching the ball curve up. Then, quick as flash, she leapt up and grabbed it with her front paws.

"Hooray! World's cleverest cat!" cried Rosy.

"I'd better see what Bonny's doing," said Tilly.

She crawled outside again and stood up, brushing herself down. Then, tucking her dress into her knickers, she pulled off her sandals and socks and slipped into the stream. Bonny had waded over to the opposite bank and was scrambling out.

"What is it, Bonny Bonbons?" called Tilly as Bonny ran over to a tree and started to scrabble furiously in the ground with her front paws. Her little bottom stuck up in the air, wiggling from side to side with sheer pleasure.

Rosy popped her head out of the tent and called, "Everything all right?"

Tilly shrugged. "Look at Bonny – she's having so much fun, isn't she?" They both laughed as Bonny sat up on her haunches and let out a loud whuff and then burrowed down to start digging again.

"Just coming up for air," said Rosy.

"I'll go and see what she's found," said Tilly, and waded back into the stream.

She was about to climb out when she heard Rosy cry out, "Tinkerbell's gone!"

Oh no! thought Tilly, and she turned round and splashed back. "She can't have gone far."

Rosy was pulling up the flaps of the sheet, hunting for Tinkerbell, and then she started tearing at undergrowth around the trees, calling, "Tinkerbell, come here, you'll get lost in the woods, please come back."

"Me and Bonny will search this way," said Tilly, whistling for her dog. "You stay here in case she's nearby."

Rosy nodded and Tilly could see she was close to tears as she continued to shake the bushes and call for her cat.

Tilly set off towards the deeper part of the wood, poking gently in the undergrowth with a stick, Bonny nosing the ground beside her. "We've got to find her, Bons," muttered Tilly. "She's absolutely essential to Rosy, isn't she?"

Bonny stopped for a second and stared up at Tilly, her brown eyes wide, ears perked as if she understood every word.

Then suddenly she gave a sharp whuff and leapt forward. Sprinting behind, Tilly saw her come to a halt in front of a huge pine tree, with branches like steps all the way up the trunk. Bonny sat down and barked and barked, her nose pointing up into the tree.

CHAPTER 2

"She's there!" cried Tilly, spotting Tinkerbell sitting on a branch licking her paws as if she didn't have a care in the world.

"Rose! Over here! Bonny's found her!" cried out Tilly, and Rosy came crashing through the bushes, bits of leaves and twigs tangled in her curly hair.

"Oh thank goodness," said Rosy, panting hard. "I love you for ever, Bonny," and she grabbed the little dog and kissed her on the nose. Bonny struggled away, giving an impatient yelp.

"I'll go up and get her," said Tilly, and she started to climb up the tree, which was quite easy. But just as she reached Tinkerbell's branch the tabby cat stood up, stretched herself and jumped off the branch, down into Rosy's waiting arms.

"She's safe, oh my poor dear little cat," cooed Rosy, burying her face in the golden fur.

"I should jolly well hope so," called out Tilly, swinging herself down to the ground.

"I'll never let you out of my sight again," murmured Rosy, the cat purring gently in her arms.

Good thing we found her, thought Tilly, as they set off back to the den. Rosy's Mum and Dad had given her Tinkerbell as a tiny kitten the year before they died. Tinkerbell was the centre of attention for months as they all discussed what to feed her and how to house-train her. Her dear little pet was one of Rosy's last links back to those happy times.

Tilly felt a tear come to her eye, and she brushed it away so that her friend wouldn't see.

They spent the rest of the afternoon playing with their pets and rearranging the hut.

"I'm trying to persuade Dad to give me this big metal box he keeps in the shed for nails and things," said Tilly, as she tweaked the corner of a sack. "It would be perfect for keeping supplies in."

"Like biscuits—"

"—and pet food and stuff."

"Then we could make our own little meals," said Rosy. "In fact, I'm pretty sure I could make a camp fire to cook potatoes and things. There's a book in the library on making fires in the outdoors."

"Wouldn't it be wonderful to camp out here properly one night?"

Rosy stared at Tilly and said, "It is absolutely *impossible* to imagine Megan agreeing to *camping*."

They rolled their eyes at each other and burst into high-pitched laughter.

"You could ask Donald to come and keep an eye on us."

"Well, he'd be lots of fun, but never in a million years would Donald go camping. Come on, we've got fifteen minutes to get home for tea."

They scurried around, gathering their things, and set off, pushing through the thicket. The sun was still quite high in the sky, and the corn in the fields was waving like a huge green sea in the breeze.

Only a few more days of freedom before school starts next week, thought Tilly, as she stood up on her pedals and raced towards the canal.

Or the war starts this week.

The war.

That's all the grown-ups had talked about this summer. She overheard Mum and Dad murmuring in the living room every evening as she went upstairs to bed.

"They won't call you up, Wilf, not again – you did your bit last time in the trenches," Mum had said the night before, in that worried voice she used these days.

"They'll call us all up and never mind the trenches," Dad had growled.

Tilly didn't know much about what Dad had done in the last war. He never talked about it. None of the fathers did.

But my Dad's not scared of anything, she told herself, pedalling over the bridge. She couldn't imagine Dad, with his big muscles and long legs, ever being afraid.

She and Rosy parted at the corner and Tilly rode on to her house, wheeling her bike up the path and propping it in the side passage near the bin. She pulled her key out of the front of her dress, where it hung on a string around her neck, and opened the front door, letting Bonny run in first.

"Go and wash your hands and then lay the table," Mum called from the kitchen. "You're late. Dad's home already."

Tilly ran upstairs, Bonny hot on her heels, and went into the bathroom to wash her hands and drag a hairbrush through her long, tangled hair. She stared for a second in the mirror. I wish it was curly like Rosy's – then I wouldn't need to brush it so much, she thought with a sigh. It's such a nuisance.

"Tilly?"

CHAPTER 2

She went out of the bathroom to see Dad on the upstairs landing. There was something in the look on his face which sent a chill through her: sort of sad and angry at the same time.

Dad's hair was brown like hers, and he kept it clipped very short. They both had dark eyebrows, brown eyes and long narrow faces like their long legs. Mum had dusty blond hair and a round face, with a dimple in one cheek. These days, she was always wiping the back of her hand across her forehead, as if everything was too much for her.

Has something happened? Tilly wondered.

She scooped up Bonny in her arms and blurted out, "Has the war started, Dad? Do me and Bonny have to go away?"

There had been a lot of talk of evacuating the children into the countryside, but Tilly hadn't taken much notice. She was too busy with the secret den.

Dad looked puzzled for a second, and then he said the words that Tilly would never forget for the rest of her life.

"The war will start very soon and dogs won't cope with the bombing and the blackout. Tomorrow I'm taking Bonny to the vet to be put down. It's the kindest thing."

Then he turned on his heel and went downstairs.

Chapter 3

TINKERBELL TOO

Sunday evening, 27th August 1939

Tilly stood at the top of the stairs, Bonny nuzzling her hand, and stared down to the hallway and the front door below. She couldn't believe what Dad had just said. How could anyone possibly want to kill her beautiful little dog?

Bonny gave a whimper. Tilly turned her head and stared down, too numb to move.

"No one's doing anything to you," whispered Tilly. "We've been together since you were born, and Daddy won't touch a hair on your head – that's a promise."

As if satisfied, Bonny stopped whimpering, sat on her bottom, and looked up with such a trusting look that Tilly's eyes filled with tears.

Then, in a surge of rage, she grabbed the banisters, swung herself downstairs four steps at a time, and landed with a roar on the hall carpet.

Mum put her head round the kitchen door. "Don't make such a noise – and you still haven't laid the table for tea."

"Is that all you can think about?" cried Tilly, marching into the kitchen.

Dad was sitting in his usual place at the top of the table, reading the evening paper. The words Poland, Germany and Government seemed to be in headlines all over the front page.

"Go and help your mother," said Dad, not looking up.

"Does Mum know about Bonny?" said Tilly, in a shaky voice.

"Know what?" said Mum.

"Dad's going to kill Bonny tomorrow!" Then her bottom lip drooped down and she burst into tears.

Mum was slicing cucumber, but she hesitated and looked at Tilly, her face dark with worry, the dimple-like creases on her pale cheek. "Now, now, " she said.

"Is tha… tha… that all you c… c… can s… say?" Tilly managed to force out between sobs.

Dad put down his paper and said, "Your mother and I agree, everyone is doing the same, dogs will go mad if there's bombing—"

"—and gas," said Mum. "Mrs Benson opposite, you know, her Alec works at the zoo." Dad nodded. "Well, she says we could face hordes of frenzied dogs rampaging through the streets, foaming at the mouth."

"And there'll be rationing; there won't be enough food for dogs and cats and the like," said Dad.

"But you don't know there'll be a war!" Tilly was almost shouting. "You can't kill my darling Bonny Bonbons – how can you even *think* about it? I've had her since she was a puppy. She's our loyal pet, and our friend! Are you going to kill all your friends if there's a war?"

Dad gave a snort as if to say "don't be ridiculous", and his eyebrows furrowed with annoyance, which made Tilly even more furious. She felt as though her head could explode with rage. It was all she could do to stop herself sweeping everything off the tea table.

They must listen, they have to listen. "How can you be so cruel! Don't you care about Bonny, don't you care about me?"

CHAPTER 3

There was a shocked silence as Mum wrung her hands together, cheeks hot and red, strands of hair sticking to her forehead. Dad dropped his eyes for a few seconds. Then he looked back up at Tilly and held up the paper.

"Look at the headlines, my girl. We have to face facts. Hitler wants Poland now. Britain and France won't let him get away with that. He's already taken other countries. He's a menace, he wants all of Europe. The whole country's preparing for war. I've dug our Anderson shelter into the garden, your mother's making blackout curtains and you'll be evacuated next Tuesday to the countryside with your friends from the High School."

"Evacuated? Wh... wh... where? Who will I stay with?" This was the first time Tilly had heard definitely that she was being sent away. A cold shiver went through her.

Mum was dabbing her eyes with her apron.

"You don't want me to go away, Mum, do you?" said Tilly, and the tears started to spurt out again.

But Mum turned to the sink and banged the pots around like she did whenever she was upset. "All the children are going. We'll pack your things this week."

"But… but… what if I hate it? Anyway, Bonny can come with me, can't she? There's no need to separate us if I'm going away. There won't be any bombs or gas in the countryside." She suddenly felt a corner of hope. Of course, that's the answer to everything.

But Dad frowned and his brown eyes narrowed as he snapped, "Don't be such a silly girl! The families who take in the evacuees won't want their pets too. I'm taking Bonny to the vet after work tomorrow, and that's my last word."

Tilly stared down at her lap, tears plopping on her napkin. What on earth am I going to do? she thought, all kinds of insane ideas running through her mind.

Mum was putting ham and salad onto plates, when suddenly there was a loud bang outside the open window. The sound of sobbing floated across the gardens.

"What was that?" said Tilly.

She glanced at her mother whose eyes were wide with fright.

"Ted Bow," said Dad, taking a slice of bread and butter. "Said he was going to shoot their greyhound with his old rifle. Eat up now, Tilly. Don't waste food."

CHAPTER 3

It's really happening, thought Tilly, feeling icy all over. They're killing the pets.

She could hardly eat anything, and for once Mum didn't insist she clear her plate. All she could think about was running round to Rosy's and collapsing in tears on her bed.

After tea Tilly asked if she could take Bonny for a walk. "I might call on Rosy," she said, trying to sound as casual as possible.

"Well, just for half an hour," said Mum. "I need you to help me with the curtains in the bedrooms. There's still so much to do and the blackout starts on Friday."

Clipping Bonny's lead on, Tilly went out of the house and down the garden path, her leg still shaking with the shock. How could everything have changed so much since they were playing in their den?

Tilly hadn't properly believed in the war up until now, although she had already decided she would be a nurse, and Rosy, who knew Morse code, wanted to work in intelligence. She'd taught Tilly the code for SOS:

ditditdit

daahh/daahh/daahh

ditditdit

But what use was cleaning wounds and breaking codes if all the pets were going to be killed?

We have to stop them, Tilly told herself, as she ran round to Rosy's house, Bonny loping at her side. She couldn't help wondering about Tinkerbell, but then she told herself, after everything Rosy had been through surely Megan wouldn't want to upset her by getting rid of her darling pet.

But she knew the minute the door opened and she saw Rosy's white face, her small frame trembling as she gripped the handle for support.

"Megan's putting Tinkerbell down tomorrow," whispered Rosy, looking over her shoulder. "What about Bonny?"

"Same," said Tilly. "Did you hear that gun go off?"

Rosy nodded. "What was it?"

"Ted Bow shot his greyhound."

Rosy stifled a sob and then pulled Tilly in through the front door, calling out, "It's only Tilly, we're going to play in my room."

They ran upstairs and once in the bedroom with the door closed, Rosy dropped onto the bed, where Tinkerbell was pawing away at the eiderdown. Bonny settled herself on the floor, nose resting on her paws, eyes fixed on Tilly.

"What are we going to do?" cried out Rosy in a loud whisper. "They can't kill our pets, they just can't."

Tilly shook her head. "I know. It's unbelievable! I told Dad he was cruel."

"I had hysterics and Donald had to calm me down, but Megan just sat there buttering the bread for tea. How can she not care? Mummy and Daddy would never have said such a terrible thing—" Her voice broke into a sob.

Tilly put her arm round her friend, and, for a few moments, all they could do was sob and clutch each other.

Then Tilly pulled herself upright and swept back her long hair from her forehead. She started to pace up and down the room, hands on her hips. "I don't care what the grown-ups think," she said, "they're just plain wrong!"

"Ab... ab... absolutely," hiccupped Rosy through her tears. "But what can we do?"

"We come up with a plan. This is our war too; we'll have to think of something before the morning."

"Well we can try, I suppose."

There was silence for a few minutes and then Tilly said, "What about asking one of the other children if they could take Tinkerbell and Bonny?"

"Why would they? The same thing's going to happen to them. Donald says the war will start by the weekend and the bombs could drop straight away. The grown-ups think the dogs will go mad and run round biting everyone."

"I would *never* let Bonny do that," said Tilly, in a shocked voice.

"Of course not, but the grown-ups won't listen. Megan goes on and on about food, how there'll be rationing and there won't be anything spare for pets."

"But Donald's a butcher. He can always get something for Tinks, can't he? Maybe you could save a bit for Bonny."

"Course," said Rosie. "Food's not the problem right now. It's saving our pets from instant death."

They sat in silence for a bit, both thinking hard, and then Rosy said, "If only we could hide them."

"Good idea, but where?"

"Your garden shed?"

"No," said Tilly, still pacing up and down. "Bonny would howl if she was locked up all night, and Dad would hear. It'd have to be somewhere further away, where no one would hear them. But how would we hide them for weeks and weeks?"

"You mean months – the war won't be over in weeks."

Tilly nodded. "They thought the last war would be over by Christmas, and it went on for four years. My Dad thinks he'll end up in the trenches again."

"Donald's OK with his one leg shorter than the other – the army wouldn't even take him last time."

"But it's not that my Dad's scared of going to war – he's not a coward," said Tilly, raising her voice.

"No! Of course not – it's just, well, he's seen things. Donald talks about it a bit: what his older brother told him before he was killed."

There was a pause, and then Rosy murmured, "I don't know what a bomb sounds like, do you?"

Tilly shook her head. "Mum looks very frightened these days whenever they talk about the war." She didn't add that she felt quite scared at the thought of a bomb dropping on their house. Would their shelter really be able to keep them safe?

Tinkerbell stretched herself and padded over to Rosy, who was sitting on the end of the bed, legs curled under her. The tabby cat stepped delicately onto her lap and settled one paw on her chest, rubbing her head against Rosy's woolly cardigan.

"Yes, my angel, what is it?" murmured Rosy, bending her head, her curly hair settling over the cat's golden fur.

"Just because they had a horrible time in the last war," declared Tilly, sounding braver than she felt, "that's no reason to murder our pets. We've got to hide them, and we've only got tomorrow to decide where and get everything ready."

"But even if we do find a hiding place, what shall we tell the grown-ups?" Rosy's anxious face stared at Tilly, who had crouched down to play with Bonny's ears.

"Oh, that's easy," said Tilly. "We tell them our pets knew that they were going to be killed, and they've run away."

For the first time, Rosy's green eyes – almost like her cat's, Tilly often thought – lit up. "That's marvellous! That's just what we'll do – and you know what? I've got a perfect idea where we can hide Tinkerbell and Bonny."

"Where?"

"Our den in the woods. It just needs a bit of fixing up: find some straw for them to lie on; make sure they can't escape. What do you think?"

Tilly leapt to her feet and Bonny started jumping up to nudge her hand. "It's a smashing idea. You're a complete and utter genius, Rosie Wilson. I *knew* we'd come up with a plan. Now here's what we do. Straight after breakfast tomorrow, we take the pets to the den. Then we have all day to make them nice and comfy before we have to go home to face the music."

"I can't wait to see Megan's face when I tell her Tinkerbell has disappeared!"

"Me too," said Tilly.

Dad will be furious when I tell him, thought Tilly, pushing out her lower lip. But I don't care. That'll teach him to even think about killing my darling Bonny Bonbons.

Chapter 4

IS ANYWHERE SAFE?

Monday 28th August 1939

"I'll do it straight after work, before tea, Mother," said Tilly's Dad at breakfast the next morning. "Make sure you have Bonny ready."

Tilly nodded, eyes fixed on her plate.

"Don't go far today," Dad went on as he stood up and pushed his chair back. "Your mother needs help in the house."

But as soon as she could, Tilly made her escape. Her bike, which Dad had bought second hand for Mum after they were married, had a big wicker basket on the front. She packed it with Bonny's special blanket and a chipped bowl from the cupboard for water, which she hoped Mum wouldn't miss. She'd wrapped up some scraps from last night's tea so that Bonny could have supper tonight.

CHAPTER 4

It'll take us all day to get the den ready, Tilly thought, as she cycled to the bridge over the canal to meet Rosy. I do wish Mum would stop nagging me to help with the blackout curtains. Honestly, how many do we need?

"Coo-ee!"

It was Rosy, waving to her from the bridge, and soon they were speeding across the waste ground between the old factories and over the field, until they reached the wood. They arrived breathless and Bonny flopped down, panting like mad.

"She needs a drink," said Tilly.

Rosy went into the hut while Tilly unpacked the bowl and took it down to the stream. Slipping off her sandals and socks and tucking her dress into her knickers, she paddled to the middle to get Bonny the freshest water.

Can't have her getting ill now, she thought. Bonny can cope with being a bit hungry, but dogs need buckets of water.

Once back on the bank, she picked up her socks and sandals, padded barefoot back to the clearing, and put the water down.

"Have you decided where to put Tinks for the night?" called out Tilly as she went into the hut.

Rosy was sitting on a crate, Tinkerbell asleep on her lap.

"I've made her a specially nice bed," said Rosy, nodding to a folded sack on the earthy floor. A snowy white handkerchief was laid at one end.

Megan would be furious if she saw that, thought Tilly.

"Only I have to actually shut her up or she'll wander off and get lost again," said Rosy. Her voice seemed more strained than usual.

Bonny was jumping up, bumping Tilly's hand with her nose, as if to say, "Any food?" Tilly pulled a dog biscuit out of her pocket, and Bonny seized it as if she was starving and crunched it down. "I'll need to tie Bonny up too. She won't like that."

Rosy was feeling her cat's forehead and now she said, "I think Tinkerbell might have a cold."

Tilly tossed her hair out of her eyes and looked over at the cat. Her golden fur did look rather limp this morning. "Oh dear," she said. "Has she eaten anything? Feed a cold, starve a fever, that's what Mum always says."

"I've got a half a sardine left over from yesterday. Do you want to hold her while I get some water?"

"I'll go, you stay with Tinks."

Bonny followed as Tilly walked back to the stream.

Out here in the clear air, with the birds singing and the insects zooming around, all thoughts of war seemed very far away. But Tilly knew from listening to the grown-ups that there was an airstrip a few miles north of their den, and everyone said the Germans could bomb anywhere. Their streets in West London were no safer than the docks over in the East End.

Is anywhere safe in a war? Tilly wondered as she climbed back onto the bank with Tinkerbell's water.

The little cat seemed to revive, and even nibbled a bit of the sardine. Rosy kept her tucked under her arm as they worked in the hut, getting everything ready for the night.

"I think I'll tie Bonny up in that corner – it's the least draughty bit," said Tilly.

"Good idea," said Rosy. "There's lots of long grass in the clearing you can put down for her bed."

"I brought her special blanket so that something smells of home."

Tilly picked up the broom and bashed away at some new cobwebs which had appeared. Then she picked a huge armful of grass and arranged it in a nice heap. But, as soon as she'd finished, Bonny scampered over and nosed through the mound, scattering it everywhere.

"Oh well," sighed Tilly. "I suppose she's not ready for bed yet."

Rosy had turned over the biggest crate and now she half-filled it with grass and laid the sack and handkerchief on top. Then she lowered Tinkerbell carefully down. The cat was asleep again.

"I just have to think how to cover it over without blocking all the air," said Rosy.

"Hmm, let's look about outside and see if we can find anything useful."

They went round to the back of the hut, where all sorts of things had been thrown down – broken farm tools, a bucket with a huge hole in the bottom, broken planks of wood and a large jumbled heap of rope and string.

"Look," pointed Tilly, her sharp eyes spotting something wiry. She started to pull at the heap. "I think it's chicken-wire, but it's stuck," she puffed, pulling hard.

Rosy grabbed one corner and they pulled together, but it was no use. They straightened and Tilly wiped her forehead with a corner of her skirt. A muddy streak appeared on the paisley cloth. "Oh bother," she muttered and rubbed hard, making it much worse. "Right, we have to dig that lot up."

"What with?"

Tilly thought for a minute, and then she went into the hut and came out with the broken broom. She inserted the handle into the heap under the wire and levered down hard. "Help me, Rose."

Rosy added all her strength to the broken stick and, with their hands slippery with sweat, they gave one last heave.

"Done it!" cried Tilly, as the pile moved away, revealing a tangle of chicken-wire.

She bent down and grabbed a piece. "This should do – and we can use some of the string to tie it in place."

By the time they had finished Tinkerbell's cage and Tilly had chosen a strong piece of rope from the heap for Bonny, they were ready for their sandwiches. They sat in the sunshine in the clearing, and then Tilly said something which had been on her mind all morning. "I do think this is a good idea – but for how long?"

"What do you mean?"

"Well, Dad says the High School is being evacuated next Tuesday—"

"—what!" Rosy's eyes were wide with surprise. "I didn't know that. Megan hasn't said anything yet."

The girls stared at each other for a minute, and then Rosy said, "Can't we take our pets? That would solve everything."

"Dad says the people looking after us wouldn't want them."

"Oh."

They sat in silence for a few minutes. Then Tilly said, "So we have to think about what we're going to do with Bonny and Tinks when we go away."

Rosy stared off into the distance and murmured, "There's no point even asking Megan. We have to find a way, Tills, we have to."

"I know."

But Tilly didn't have a clue where to start. If everyone is going to kill their pets, as Dad said, then who on earth could they ask for help?

After lunch, they decided to test out the night-time arrangements for the pets. Tilly clipped Bonny's lead onto her collar and pushed a piece of thick rope through the loop at the end of the lead. She'd found a length on the heap – long enough for Bonny to stand up and walk a few steps, but that was all.

She tied the other end of the rope to a post sticking out of the wall, using a figure of eight, which Dad always said was the strongest knot. Bonny started to whine the minute she was put on the lead, and now, as Tilly pulled down hard on the rope to make sure it wouldn't come loose, the little dog began a sharp whuff, building up to a full-blown bark.

"I know, my darling," Tilly said. "But you have to put up with it – it's only at night, I promise."

Bonny wasn't listening. The barking at first just a query, and then a hurt comment punctuated with yelps, had turned into a steady, loud, continuous bark.

How far away can she be heard? Tilly wondered.

"I'm going to the field," she said to Rosy, who was still fixing the chicken-wire for Tinkerbell's cage. "To see if I can hear Bonny barking."

Rosy nodded, her tongue curling up the side of her mouth as she wrestled with the wire.

Tilly went outside and pushed through the thicket, Bonny's barks ringing in her ears, and set off at a jog across the field. The barks didn't really become too faint until she was in the middle of the field, but as she almost reached the factories, they died away completely.

It will have to do, she told herself, and jogged back.

"It's time to go," said Rosy, looking at her watch as Tilly appeared again in the hut.

The moment they had been dreading had finally arrived. They would have to leave their pets for the whole night, and if anything happened to them…

Tilly could hardly bear to think about it.

"Is the wire all right?" she asked, delaying the final moment.

Rosy nodded. "Tinkerbell's sleeping a lot at the moment anyway with her cold, so I don't think she'll try and escape."

Tilly went over to Bonny, who'd stopped barking and was looking up at her as if to say, "I've had enough of this game, let's go home now."

"Not tonight, my darling," she said, bending down for a kiss. She smoothed the curly ears against Bonny's face as her dog put out her tongue and licked her cheek.

The sun had already gone behind the wood and the light had faded in the hut. It felt a cold, ghostly place to be locked away in for a whole night, and for many nights to come, perhaps.

"Don't be too frightened and lonely," she whispered.

"She has Tinkerbell for company," said Rosy, in a small voice. "We have to go and tell our stories about them running away. I'm absolutely dreading it – Megan will go mad."

Tilly was feeling quite scared too. What would Dad say? Would he guess and make her go to the hut and get Bonny?

"Better get it over with," she said, and the two girls walked slowly backwards out of the hut, blowing kisses all the way and wiping their eyes.

Bonny started to bark, punctuated with high-pitched, heart-breaking yelps. Tilly could hear her all the way across the field. She nearly turned back, but only the thought of the terrible fate which lay in front of her pet kept her going.

As she arrived home, her legs feeling weak and wobbly, Dad was coming down the stairs.

"Where's Bonny?" he said. "It's time."

He was dangling a lead like a hangman's rope from his hand.

Chapter 5

THE EMERGENCY ZOO

Monday evening to Tuesday 29th August 1939

Dad was silent all through tea. Mum fussed around with her worried look on her face. Tilly ate as little as possible, sneaking bits of food onto her lap whenever no one was looking. Finally, sliding her napkin under the table and wrapping the food up, she said, "May I be excused please?"

"Where's your gas mask?" Dad barked at her. "Or is that lost too?"

"I... no... of course not," muttered Tilly.

"Well it's a funny thing, Mother, isn't it? The very day I say the dog's going to the vet she runs away."

Mum nodded but she didn't say anything.

"Then Donald tells me when I stop by the shop for a word on the way home from work today that Rosy's cat

Tinkerbell is missing," Dad goes on. "So what do you have to say for yourself, my girl?"

"Rosy and I searched and searched everywhere for Bonny. I'm sure she'll come home soon, Dad." The tears which Tilly had been holding back spurted out of her eyes and she buried her face in her napkin. "I l... l... love Bonny so much and now she's... she's... gone."

Mum got up and pulled Tilly's head against her apron. Tilly sniffed in the familiar cooking smells.

"There, there, my love," Mum murmured. "Dad and I don't mean to be cruel. Do we, Dad?"

"No, of course not," said Dad, in a kinder voice.

When Tilly looked up, she could see his ears had gone bright red, which they always did when he was upset.

He does feel sorry, she thought, and she almost blurted out the truth.

But then Dad said, "We have no choice, we can't keep a pet through the war, can we, Mother?"

Mum shook her head and wiped a tear away with a corner of her apron.

Nothing will change their minds, Tilly realized, and she knew she would have to keep this secret now for the whole of the war – perhaps for years and years.

As she lay in bed that night, she tried to imagine Bonny in the cold, gloomy hut. She must think I've abandoned her for ever, was her last thought as she fell asleep.

Tuesday morning was bright and sunny as Tilly raced outside after breakfast, grabbed her bike and pedalled to meet Rosy on the bridge. Without a word, they both rode as fast as they could to their den.

Bonny was barking as they threw their bikes down in the clearing. Tilly ran through the door, Rosy puffing behind her, and grabbed her dog, who was almost strangling herself as she jumped and pulled against the rope.

"Bonny darling, you're all right. Thank goodness." Bonny leapt into Tilly's arms, her big, rough tongue licking and licking all over her cheeks and nose. Tilly breathed in the musky smell and wondered how on earth she could ever leave Bonny alone again. It had been so hard to fall asleep last night without her dear little dog flopped across her legs.

Rosy was murmuring to Tinkerbell. "Good morning, my angel, are you going to give me a morning kiss?"

Tilly released Bonny, who started to bark and run outside, waiting at the door and barking some more. She didn't want to let Tilly out of her sight, even to relieve herself in the clearing.

"Is Tinks all right?" asked Tilly, holding back for a second.

"She's still sleeping, but she's warm and cosy," said Rosy, pulling the cat onto her lap and kissing her button nose. "You go out with Bonny."

Relieved, Tilly raced outside, and when Bonny was ready, they ran down to the stream for a paddle and a drink. All her fears of the night before had vanished the minute she saw her beloved pet.

"Bonny Bonbons, I love you!" she shouted with joy, and Bonny paused in her lapping to whuff back.

As they walked back to the hut after a long drink and a play in the water, Tilly heard the sound of whooping and laughter, and then bikes broke through the thicket and into the clearing.

Someone yelled, "Wotcha, Tills."

Oh no, groaned Tilly to herself. It was Neville Scudder from Canal Street school. Neville was twelve like Tilly and Rosy, and he had his younger brother and sister, Sidney and Pam, with him.

Sidney, who was ten, with untidy fair hair like all the Scudders, and bony legs poking through patched grey shorts, skidded to a halt in front of Tilly and leapt off his bike. It was too big for him to do anything else.

"Oi, Nev, let's build a fire right 'ere."

"Shut up," panted Neville, as he pulled up his brakes.

Pam, who was only seven, pulled up next to him, sniffing, her face smudged with tears. She wore a cardigan which was too small for her and unravelling around the hems, a patched grey skirt and plimsolls with no socks. None of the Scudders ever looked as if they had a bath or even a wash.

"Tilly," called out Pam. "Nev says you gonna save our pets." Then she let out a big sob.

Neville told her to shut up.

Rosy came out of the hut, cuddling Tinkerbell, her eyebrows knitted in a deep frown.

"How did you find us?" Tilly said to Neville.

"Followed you. You keeping your pets 'ere? The grown-ups wanna kill 'em."

Neville was not quite as tall as Tilly, and was very thin. Tilly remembered seeing him once at the swimming pool, and all his ribs stuck out either side of his narrow chest.

CHAPTER 5

The Scudders lived by the canal near their school. Tilly's mum had told her there was a new baby and their mother was very unwell.

"You're not to go near those children," Mum told her with a frown. "You'll catch nits, scabies, all sorts."

But Tilly and Rosy thought the Scudders were good fun and they were quite fearless. Only, could they keep a secret?

"Well," said Tilly. "This is our den, we've had it all summer and it's private."

"But we've got to save the guineas and Clover," wailed Pam, and she burst into more loud sobs.

"Dad says they're for the pot," said Sidney.

"You can't eat guinea pigs," said Tilly.

"Actually, you can," said Rosy. "They raise them in South America. They eat them like we eat rabbits."

"You can't eat Clover, you can't," wailed Pam. "Because I love 'im and I told Miss Cotton I wouldn't never let nothing 'appen to 'im."

She reached into the large basket on the front of Neville's bike and pulled aside an old piece of sacking. Nestling in some rather soiled-looking newspaper were two guinea pigs and a plump brown rabbit with a white bob-tail. Pam grabbed the rabbit by the scruff of his neck and picked him up, cuddling him in her arms.

"Goodness," said Rosy. "Looks like you're trying to hang him."

"'E likes it," said Pam.

"They're from the school," said Neville. "Pam offered to look after 'em for the 'olidays, dunno why—"

"—because I love 'em!"

"I said shut up!" Neville shook his fist towards Pam. "Anyways," he went on, "the school don't want 'em back, what with the war about to start. Miss Cotton came round last night and told Dad. He reckons we can cook 'em, but Pam…" He raised his eyebrows and propped his bike up against a tree.

"Bet I could sell 'em for a shilling," said Sidney.

"Not if you want to see Christmas," said Pam, giving him a hard stare. "Please, Tilly, can't you look after our pets?"

"We couldn't possibly—" started Tilly.

"Yes, of course we can," said Rosy. "We have to save the pets from the grown-ups before there are no more animals left on this earth. So now we have one cat, one dog, two guinea pigs and a rabbit."

Tilly was just about to say that was more than enough when she heard a cheery whistle and, looking over to the thicket, she saw Mrs Benson's Alec appear, carrying what looked like a fish tank.

"Neville said something about a hiding place for pets. I need you to take Freddy."

Alec lowered the tank gently to the ground. He wore a peaked cap, a thick blue jacket with shiny buttons and heavy boots. Alec was fifteen and had just started work in London Zoo.

"Where did you get him?" asked Tilly, peering in through the glass wall of the tank. All she could see was leaves and twigs.

"The zoo. They're turning off the heat in the reptile house tomorrow, so all the poisonous snakes and spiders and suchlike will die," said Alec.

"Good thing too," muttered Neville.

"How can you say such a thing!" cried Rosy, stepping forward, her green eyes flashing. "A snake has just as much right to live as any other animal, and so do spiders and lions and tigers and all the animals."

"Well, I agree but—" began Tilly, but Alec interrupted with a snort.

"Now look here, if the zoo gets bombed and the pythons escape—"

"Cor!" said Sidney.

"—he'd swallow that nice cat of yours whole," Alec finished.

Rosy stuck her chin in the air and said, "Well what about the elephants and the lions and tigers? They could run around trampling on people and eating them—"

"—and goring them to death," cried Sidney. He picked up a stick and stabbed it in the air. "We could play gladiators!"

"Shut up," said Neville.

"It is a crying shame," agreed Alec. "Some of the snakes are rare and you should see the markings on them. Right beautiful they are. I ain't got anything against any living creature. We all feel the same in the zoo. Very upset some of the older men are, I can tell you. We got bird-eating spiders and scorpions, all sorts. But Head Keeper says if a bomb falls on the zoo, the poisonous animals could escape and kill people. He says they won't kill the Komodo dragon. They'll move him and all the big animals out to places like Whipsnade in the countryside, so don't worry about the elephants and suchlike."

"That's a relief," said Tilly. "So what's in your tank?"

"Freddy," said Alec. "Saw him being born only last Saturday, so I couldn't let them have him."

"What is he?" asked Rosy, coming over to peer in the tank.

"Baby cobra."

"What!" Rosy gave out a squeal and stepped back.

"He's quite safe and I'll look after him," said Alec. "Please take him, Tilly, I can't let him die."

"Looks like the zoo's moved to the woods, ain't it, Tills?" said Sidney.

Tilly exchanged looks with Rosy, who gave her a firm nod.

Tilly puffed her cheeks out, and then, folding her arms, she said, "Well, I suppose we're the emergency zoo."

They all cheered and Alec pushed his cap onto the back of his head with a grin.

Then Rosy said in what Tilly called her "Megan voice", "That's all very well, but we have to keep this a deadly secret, or our zoo won't last long."

"What if we want to help other kids here save their pet?" asked Alec.

"We're full," muttered Neville.

"No we ain't. This place is almost as big as our classroom," said Sidney.

Tilly was thinking hard, and now she said, "We need a password so that only people we trust will know about our emergency zoo."

"I was thinking the same thing – and I've got one," said Rosy. "*Doof tep.* It's 'pet food' backwards."

"That's it," said Tilly. "Right, everyone, you can tell a child where to come if they need to hide a pet, and give them the password. We'll take turns keeping lookout in the thicket. Anyone who comes near has to say the password before we let them see the den."

Everyone agreed and Rosy said, "We'd better get the pets settled for the night."

They set to work, laughing and chattering as they made the den ready. Pam pulled up great swathes of fresh grass and filled up a crate for the guinea pigs, and another for the rabbit. Neville and Sidney found the chicken-wire around the back of the hut, and they put this over the top of each crate, tied down with pieces of string.

"That'll stop the foxes, eh Tills?" said Sidney.

Pam started to wail again: Neville told her to shut up.

Alec's tank was given a place in a dark corner.

"I've got to keep Freddy warm until I work out what to do with him," Alec told Tilly.

"What does he eat?"

Alec grinned and pulled a dead rat out of his pocket. Tilly gasped but was pleased with herself that she didn't scream. Alec was fifteen, and she didn't want him to think she was a cry-baby. A zoo keeper, even a beginner zoo keeper, would be useful.

Alec pushed aside the heavy metal lid on top of the tank and dropped the rat in. Freddy didn't move.

"Maybe he's not hungry," said Tilly.

"He's cold now. I'll come round in the morning and take him out in the sun for a bit. He'll soon wake up and start eating. You'll see."

"I want to see too," said Sidney, leaning forward.

"Now you listen, nipper," said Alec, turning on him with a fierce look on his face. "You never ever touch this tank. If I see your fingers anywhere on the lid or anywhere *near* it, I'll cut 'em off."

Sidney stuck his chin in the air defiantly, but gave a grudging nod and shoved his hands into his pockets.

"Right then," said Alec to Tilly. "That should keep him away."

Is this war? wondered Tilly, as they biked away after another heart-breaking parting from their pets. Ted Bow shot his greyhound, Dad wants to murder Bonny and Sidney will get bitten to death if Alec doesn't almost frighten him to death.

Chapter 6

LOTTE AND RUDI

Tuesday evening, 29th August 1939

Tilly had to find her gas mask box before they sat down to tea so that Dad wouldn't have another excuse to snap at her. She finally dug it out from under her bed and, slipping the string over her shoulder, she walked downstairs and into the kitchen.

Dad was reading aloud a bit from the paper, "...and you wouldn't believe the rumours going round, Mother," he said. He spotted Tilly's gas mask and nodded. Then he went on, "Listen to this. *One woman said to another in the bus queue, 'There's gas that kills people and leaves them standing bolt upright in the middle of the street.'*"

"Oh," said Mum, "I thought that was true. Mrs Benson said as much last week."

"That would be horrible," said Tilly, with a grimace.

"For goodness' sakes, it's all stuff and nonsense, just stupid war rumours," said Dad, and he gave Tilly a broad grin. "Don't you go listening to anything that woman says. Pass the bread and butter, Tilly, and help your mother put out the cutlery."

Tilly laid the table and then she said, "I heard today that in the last war they were all saying the Russians had landed in the East End with snow on their boots."

Dad let out a laugh. "Just another rumour. Well, we're not going to lose our sense of humour just because of a stupid war, eh Mother?"

But Mum just wiped her forehead and dished up the stew.

"Do you want a war, Dad?" asked Tilly, as she wondered how on earth she could save stew and mashed potatoes for Bonny.

"No, of course not – but we have to stop Hitler, or none of us will be safe." Dad mixed gravy with his mash and then said more thoughtfully, as if he was worried he'd scared her, "But don't you worry, love, you'll be far away from it all."

CHAPTER 6

I can never stop worrying about Bonny, thought Tilly. Why can't Dad understand?

Just as they finished, a polite knock came on the front door.

"Who's that at tea time?" said Mum.

"I'll go," said Tilly, relieved to get away from the table.

She ran down the corridor and opened the front door. On the step stood a girl of about sixteen. She had very pale skin and dark shadows under her eyes, with a hunted look about her. She wore a drab white blouse and black skirt, and her hair hung neatly in two light brown plaits.

"Please, I am Lotte," said the girl, in what sounded like a German accent.

Tilly stared at her, wondering if the war had started and this was the enemy already on the doorstep. She looked up and down the street, almost expecting to see soldiers marching past, but there was only the postman delivering the last letters of the day.

"Who is it?" she heard Dad's voice thunder down the hallway.

"Please, Tilly, you must to help me. It is my poor brother, Rudi."

She dropped her arm behind her and pulled a small boy round. He had the same dark eyes with the same bruised look, and he was even paler than Lotte. He wore grey shorts and a grey school shirt, and in his arms was the sweetest little dachshund Tilly had ever seen.

"They want to kill him," whispered Lotte.

In that instant, Tilly knew she meant the dog.

She swung round and called out, "Just my friends from school, Dad. We're going to play in my room."

Before Dad could answer or come down the hallway to see who was there, Tilly put her fingers to her lips, beckoned to the children on the path, and they all ran lightly up the stairs and into Tilly's room without a word.

Tilly closed the door and let out her breath. "Phew!" she said. "That was close. We mustn't let Dad know there's a dog in the house. The grown-ups want to kill all the pets."

Rudi pressed his face into his dog's chocolate-brown fur which looked to Tilly as smooth as silk. The dog was resting his long slender nose on Rudi's arm and Tilly thought his dark eyes were almost as beautiful as

Bonny's. She wondered with a pang if Bonny was still barking for her in the hut.

"Alec Benson lives next door," Lotte was whispering. "He tells us you are keeping safe some pets. He tells us a password too, but I forget it. I am sorry, Tilly, but I come to ask you please to save Hanno." Lotte pulled Tilly over to the window. "I need Hanno to save Rudi. He does not speak since... since... we came to England. He is very homesick."

"Where are you from?" asked Tilly.

"Frankfurt." Lotte stared into Tilly's eyes and then looked away.

"Germany?"

Lotte nodded and then she looked back, saying quickly, "But we are not your enemy, Tilly, please believe me. A lot of good Germans run away from Hitler and the Nazis. They hate them like you."

"Oh," said Tilly, but she wasn't sure what to believe. What if they were spies?

Then the dachshund wriggled in Rudi's arms and gave a little sneeze, blinking his eyes as if he'd surprised himself. Tilly couldn't help laughing.

"My dog Bonny has exactly the same look when she sneezes," she said.

"Oh, you have a dog too – that is very nice," said Lotte, with a strained smile on her face. "Do you keep her in the safe place?"

"Oh yes, Dad says he wants to put her down. The grown-ups are so cruel."

Lotte nodded. "Yes, it is. Terrible, horrible." Tilly couldn't help smiling, and the older girl blushed and said, "Excuse, my English is not good but please, Tilly," she plucked Tilly's blouse as if to try and make her listen, "Rudi misses Papa and Mutti so so much. They put us on a train to England to be safe. We are not your enemy, Tilly, please to trust me. Hitler is the enemy."

They stood in complete silence for a moment. Tilly wondered if Lotte was telling the truth and then she thought, How could this brother and sister do anyone any harm? And they love their pet, just like me and Rosy.

"Did you bring Hanno with you on the train?"

"No, it is not permitted. Mutti's friend bring Hanno to England and he is put to quarantine. Now he is free and healthy but Rudi's foster parents, Mr and Mrs Evans – do you know them?"

Tilly nodded. The Evans lived opposite, further down the street, next to Alec Benson and his mum.

"They are such good people for Rudi." Lotte's eyes filled with tears again. "Mutti is very happy Rudi is in a safe home. But now the Evans say Hanno must die. They do not understand about Rudi. They say all the pets must die. But Tilly, you understand."

Lotte gripped Tilly's arm hard and locked eyes with her. Tilly didn't feel it was right to look away, even though she felt rather uncomfortable.

"Rudi starts to speak when Hanno come home," hissed Lotte, glancing over her shoulder again. "But now he stops because he is so sad. If Hanno killed, maybe Rudi never speaks again. What do I say to Mutti and Papa after the war finish? I am looking after Rudi, Mutti says I must. Please, Tilly, help me save Rudi and take Hanno to your safe place."

Tilly's head was whirling. They were Germans, but not Nazis, their parents had sent them away and Rudi was living with foster parents – but what about Lotte?

"Don't you have foster parents too?"

"I work in big house, clean kitchen, change beds. I am servant."

"Oh, didn't you want to stay at school?"

Lotte's head dropped. "I am not English girl like you, Tilly. I must work for my food. But Rudi is good boy, study in the school. And he loves Hanno too too much."

But you can't love your dear little pet too much, thought Tilly, can you? She made her mind up.

"Of course we'll take Hanno. Bring them to the bridge over the canal at nine tomorrow morning."

Lotte spun on her heel and directed an excited stream of German towards Rudi who nodded, his face buried in Hanno's neck. Then he gave a low bow and said in a small voice, "*Ja. Danke, Tilly.*"

Lotte's face lit up at the sound of Rudi's voice.

"What did he say?" asked Tilly.

"Yes, thank you." Lotte grabbed Tilly's hands and swung them to and fro. "You are good, kind girl and Papa will reward you when he comes to England."

"No need," said Tilly. "This is the children's war, saving our pets."

"Yes, you are right, the children are at war too. But now we must go."

They all went downstairs and Tilly let the brother and sister out of the front door before Mum and Dad could see them. She wasn't exactly sure what they might say about the enemy coming into the house.

As she lay in bed that night, Tilly thought about Hitler and his Nazis.

"We've got Lotte and Rudi now," she said out loud, "and they're staying right here, safe in England, with their dear little dog in our emergency zoo. So put that in your pipe and smoke it, Mr Hitler."

"*Doof tep,*" she whispered before she fell asleep.

Chapter 7

MORE AND MORE PETS

Wednesday 30th August 1939

"Where are you off to?" Mum was standing in the kitchen doorway, hands on her hips.

Tilly swivelled round just as she reached the front door. "I'm going to look for Bonny."

"You know what will happen if you bring her home."

"Yes, Dad will murder her," and ignoring her mother's gasp, Tilly went out, closing the door behind her, grabbed her bike and made off down the road.

Under her dress was a bag with bits of food for the pets. She hoped Rosy would bring some scraps from Donald too. Feeding all those pets was their biggest problem right now.

As Tilly cycled along the road, she saw a group of workmen near the park, shovelling a huge heap of sand into sacks and laying them round the public air raid shelter. Dad said there was room for a hundred people inside. The sandbags would absorb the blasts when the bombs dropped. One man was nailing up a large black sign with a white S in the middle.

S for Shelter, thought Tilly, and she wondered how fast she would have to cycle to reach the shelter if she was near the canal.

Dad had finished the Anderson shelter in their back garden, and he kept making them practise going down into it. It was damp and smelly inside and Mum said they would get pneumonia in the winter, and wasn't it a good thing the children were being evacuated. But she always said that with a catch in her voice, and Tilly knew she was dreading sending her away. If only the grown-ups would let us take our pets, can't they see how it would make everyone less homesick, she told herself for the umpteenth time.

As she reached the end of the street, she had to slow down. A line of children were snaking out of the school and crossing the road. A whistle sounded and the line stopped in front of a teacher, her cheeks red from blowing.

Tilly spotted Neville and went over to him. "What on earth are you doing?"

Neville shook his head in despair. "They keep making us come into school and practise walking to the blimmin' station for when we gets evacuated. It's the third time. They must think we're soft in the 'ead. We're not going 'til next week."

Tilly suddenly realized with a jolt that there were only seven days until she and Rosy were evacuated with the High School, as Dad had said. Feeding the zoo might be the biggest problem this morning, but they were no nearer to deciding who will look after the pets when they go away.

The teacher blew her whistle again and the children marched off.

As Tilly cycled off, she thought back to the beginning of the summer when she and Rosy had talked about being evacuated. The war had seemed so far away and unreal in July. They hadn't thought much about it as they played in their den, turning it into their own little home for themselves and their pets.

But now the coming war felt like a lion pacing its cage, ready to escape and rage out of control. As Tilly rode towards the canal, she told herself they needed a plan urgently for the emergency zoo. Time was running out.

With this new worry going round in her mind, she pedalled onto the bridge where Rudi was waiting with Hanno in his arms.

"Is Lotte coming?" she asked, as she came up alongside him.

But Rudi just kept his head bent over Hanno's chocolate-brown head.

"This way," Tilly said.

She got off her bike and walked alongside Rudi between the factories, and into the open fields. She could see a group of children up ahead with Rosy. There was a boy about her age striding along, with very short hair and a home-made bow slung over his shoulder. Behind him was a small girl of about seven pushing a bicycle. Two boys a bit older were chattering loudly and passing a cardboard box between them. Everyone was walking towards the secret den.

This won't do, she told herself. They'll give us away.

"Come on," she said to Rudi, and she ran forward to catch up with the others.

Rosy was pushing her bike along, reading a book balanced on the handlebars.

"This is a bit much," Tilly said.

Rosy's eyes stayed on her book as she said, "The new ones said the password. Sidney knows them."

"But they'll give the game away if they all walk together like this."

Rosy looked up, took in the noisy group of children and nodded. "You're right. We need some rules."

Before Tilly could reply, there was the sound of snorting and clopping behind them. Looking round, she saw a woman and a girl on horseback, both with long blond hair streaming beneath hard hats. They wore full riding kit with cream jodhpurs, black riding jackets and they each held a riding crop. The girl was on a jet-black horse and the woman was on a chestnut mare.

"What are these urchins doing beyond the canal?" the woman called out to the girl, pointing her riding crop in the direction of the line of children.

The girl, who looked older than Tilly, with a straight back and a rather haughty chin, called back, "I don't know, Mummy." But Tilly noticed her cheeks went a bit red.

"Come on, Sophia," said the mother. "We can go home the other way."

The mother began to pull on her reins, but as the girl turned her horse's head, she swivelled round and raised her eyebrows towards Tilly. They stared at each other for a moment.

Then the boy with the bow called out, "You'd better keep away from us urchins." There were sniggers from the other children and the boy planted an arrow in his bow and pulled it taut.

The girl's eyes opened wide. She gave her horse a hard kick and broke into a trot, spraying mud over Tilly's front wheel.

"Hey, look out," Tilly cried as the girl sped away.

Something whizzed through the air and an arrow fell into the grass behind the horse.

"Missed!" the boy called out.

"Get her next time!" someone jeered.

"I wonder who that was," said Tilly, joining Rosy. "Her mother's such a snob. How dare she speak to us like that!"

"Sophia Highcliffe-Barnes," said Rosy, pushing her bike as she walked beside her. "She goes to boarding school."

"Oh. What are they doing riding round here?"

"Search me. She lives a few miles away in a huge house with stables and tennis courts. Donald supplies their meat and I've been with him on delivery day in the van. I don't think Sophia—"

"*Snooty*—"

"Hmm, perhaps. Anyway, I don't think Sophia will be worrying about anyone killing *her* pets. Rich people will have somewhere to go to in the countryside, and they can take their pets with them."

"It's so unfair," said Tilly with a sigh, as they arrived at the den.

She threw her bike down and rushed into the hut to see Bonny, who was jumping up and barking wildly, her ears flying in all directions.

"Oh, my darling Bonny Bonbons," Tilly cried out as she untied the lead. "I've missed you so much."

She gathered Bonny into her arms, who started to lick and lick her face until she thought it would rub out completely.

"*Doof tep.* Where can I put Antony?" came a voice from the doorway.

It was the seven-year-old girl. She was dressed in a crisp, yellow blouse and pleated skirt, and her hair was tied in two neat pigtails with a very straight parting in the middle. In her arms, a snowy white rabbit was struggling to hop down.

Tilly laughed. "You don't need to say the password now you're in. Why don't you choose one of the wooden boxes? I'm Tilly and this is Bonny. What's your name?"

"Mary," said the girl and, giving a sniff, she said, "Mummy says Antony should always sleep in a clean cage."

"Hmm, well that's all we've got. If you want to save your rabbit—"

"Course I do! Antony is my best friend!" cried out Mary.

Tilly left her to it and went out to see what the others were doing. She spotted Rosy with Tinkerbell lying in her arms as usual. The cat's lovely golden fur which usually shone in the sunlight looked quite matted today.

Rosy had wet her handkerchief, and was dabbing it on Tinkerbell's mouth and smoothing round her eyes, which remained tightly shut. She looked rather worried, so Tilly decided to wait until later to talk about their evacuation and making a plan for the zoo.

The Scudders had arrived and Mary came out of the hut, clutching her rather fat rabbit in her arms.

"You can stroke him if you like," she said.

Tilly reached over and ran her hands over the soft white fur. She could feel the bony hip under her hand. The rabbit started to wriggle and Mary had to struggle to keep him in her arms. She'd better sit down before he jumps out and runs away, thought Tilly.

"Pam, this is Mary," she said. "Why don't you girls sit down in the grass and make a run for the rabbits and the guinea pigs with your legs. They could do with some exercise after being shut up all night in the hut."

"Ooh yes," cried out Pam, "and we can make daisy chains for 'em. Come on."

Mary looked a bit uncertain, but then she followed Pam into the den and they brought out the guinea pigs and both rabbits.

"Tilly, help us," called out Pam, her arms full with her rabbit and two of the guinea pigs. "Clover just kicked Toffee."

"Sit down over here, then," said Tilly, lifting the guinea pig out of Pam's arms. Its fur was rougher than the rabbit's and it had a musky smell. "Are you Toffee, eh, are you, little guinea?" she murmured as she stroked along its back. Toffee had light brown fur with a white face and black patches round both eyes.

They all sat down in the grass and Tilly showed the girls how to open their legs and allow the guinea pigs to run around while they held the rabbits. Sidney and the boy with the bow brought over pieces of wood and some chicken-wire and helped to build a run.

"Phew," said Mary, wiping her forehead and leaving a streak of mud, "thank goodness we can let them go. Antony was getting very upset, wasn't he?"

"So were Toffee and Apple," said Pam, stroking each of the guinea pigs in turn. "Toffee's the naughtiest – she eats all the food and Apple's the baby." Apple had black and white fur, with one brown ear. Toffee was settled in the grass, chewing away, as Apple hopped about, stretching her legs. The rabbits were feeding on a juicy pile of dandelions someone had pulled up for them.

"But we need carrots for the rabbits, don't we, Tilly?" said Mary.

Tilly nodded, getting to her feet. "We need lots of food for our pets and everyone has to help. See if you can bring a bag of vegetable peelings from home tomorrow. You can always say it's for the pig bin, like in school."

She looked around for Neville and called out, "Could you go on lookout the other side of the thicket? Make sure anyone who comes knows the password."

Neville went off.

"I'll get some chicken-wire and make a safe crate for that new rabbit, eh Tills?" said Sidney.

Tilly nodded and went off to get water for Bonny.

When she came back from the stream, she spotted a cardboard box dumped under a tree. There were air holes punched in the lid and, when she looked inside, she saw a tortoise with scaly legs poking out from under his shell. The light seemed to wake him up, and as Tilly watched, the head appeared, reaching up on its long neck. One eye opened and closed and opened again as if he was slowly winking at her.

"Hello, Mr Tortoise," said Tilly, and she picked him up carefully with both hands. The claws scrabbled a little against her palms, but she liked the cool, rough feel of the leathery skin.

"Come on," she said, "let's find your owners."

Tilly stood up and looked round for the two boys who had brought the box, but there was no sign of them.

"Sidney?" she called as Sidney came out of the hut. "What about this tortoise?"

"Oh," said Sidney, coming over with his hands in his pockets. "Thing is, Tills, them twins brought 'im cos they're going away today with their Mum to Wales. I said we could take 'im." His voice trailed off.

Tilly sighed and called out to Rosy, "What happens if they just dump their pets on us?"

Rosy was sitting with her back against a tree, offering a scrap of food to Tinkerbell. Without looking up, she said, "We look after them like our own."

"There's plenty of room in the hut for another box," said the boy with the bow, coming over. "He'll sleep all winter, anyway."

"You have to have your own pet to be here," called out Mary, in her prim little voice.

The boy pulled a white rat out from his pocket with a grin and the girls screamed. "Meet Domino. My pet's portable. He goes everywhere with me." Domino snuffled around in the boy's hand, and he pulled out a crumb from his pocket and offered it. The rat licked it up and sat up on its haunches, as if asking for more. "He's a proper little Oliver Twist," the boy laughed and put the rat back in his pocket. Then he said to Tilly, "I'll get the tortoise settled in the hut if you like."

Tilly handed the new pet over, just as a whistling sound came from the thicket.

"Who goes there? Password!" she heard Neville call out.

Tilly ran over and pushed her way through the brambles. A girl of about sixteen stood there with a bored expression on her face. At her feet was a cage containing a large green parrot with a red crown and a vicious-looking hooked beak, over an inch long.

"Oh grow up," said the girl. "You know me, Neville Scudder, you idiot." Then, seeing Tilly's frown she muttered, "*Doof tep,* all right?"

Tilly nodded. "You can come in."

"I'm not going in *there*," said the girl in disgust. "I've just brought Pirate."

Pirate gave an irritated squawk and glared at Tilly, jabbing his beak towards her. Tilly took a step back.

The girl was saying, "We've had him for years, but now Mum says he has to be put down. Alec Benson said you'd take him."

With that, she turned and walked off at a fast pace across the field.

"Wait a minute," called Tilly after her. "You need to help look after him."

But the girl didn't stop.

So this is our zoo, thought Tilly. People bring their animals and dump them on us and we have to feed them and keep them alive and I *still* don't know who will look after them when we're all evacuated.

She was beginning to wonder if the emergency zoo was such a good idea after all.

Chapter 8

WRITING IN CODE

Wednesday afternoon, 30th August 1939

"Looks like we're stuck with him," said Tilly.

Neville picked up the cage and the parrot let out a squawk.

They walked back to the clearing and Rosy came over, Tinkerbell fast asleep in her arms. "Splendid, a parrot – can he talk? *Pretty boy, pretty boy*," she tried, in a high-pitched voice – but the parrot just stared at her.

"His name's Pirate," said Tilly in a weary voice. "And they've just dumped him on us. Goodness knows what he eats."

Rosy peered in the cage again. "Look, there's a bag of seed on the floor behind him." She opened the cage and, clucking cautiously, she reached her hand inside. Pirate started to strut up and down on his perch.

"Quick, Rose, he might peck you," said Tilly.

Rosy reached a bit further, grabbed the bag and pulled it out, shutting the cage door behind her and fastening it tight. Pirate gave three loud, annoyed squawks.

"Got a lot to say for himself," muttered Tilly. She didn't think she could ever be as brave as Rosy and reach into the cage.

"At least 'e don't need a crate," said Neville. "Let's see where we can put 'im."

They went in the hut and looked around.

"How about up there?" said Tilly. She pointed to a big nail sticking out of the wall. "The other animals couldn't reach that high."

Neville put down the cage, stood on a crate, grabbed the nail and wiggled it about. It was quite loose, so he took his shoe off and banged it back in. "Pass 'im up," he called out, and he hung the cage up. "The foxes won't get 'im now," he said, jumping down.

"Who wants to see Freddy feeding?" a voice called out.

It was Alec. He came into the hut, picked up the tank and took it outside. Placing it gently on the grass, he raised the lid and poked a long stick inside.

"There he is. Ain't he a beauty?"

Tilly peered over Alec's shoulder and saw a thin, blue-brown weaving body appear from beneath the mound of bark at the bottom of the tank.

"He's five days old and already a foot long," said Alec, as Freddy raised his head and darted it from side to side. "See the markings on his head, they're called chevrons. Freddy's a King Cobra. One bite and you're dead."

A gasp went out round the children.

"What does 'e eat?" said Sidney, in a hushed voice. His face was very close to the top of the tank, and Tilly pulled him back.

Alec opened a bloody piece of rag. "He likes dead mice but I couldn't find none so I got him a nice bit of cow heart. See?"

Inside the rag were some pieces of dark red meat. The smell was revolting.

Tilly felt her stomach heave and turned her head away to watch the little girls playing with their pets. They had found some tubes and were putting the guinea pigs inside, squealing as they came out the other end.

"Apple's the bravest," said Mary.

"And Toffee's the fattest," said Pam, and they broke into giggles.

Tilly almost went over to join them. After all, you can't cuddle a snake, she thought. But she didn't want Alec to think she didn't care about Freddy, so she turned back as he dropped the pieces of meat in the tank. Freddy was darting his head around.

"Why don't 'e scoff it down?" said Sidney. He had his own stick in his hand and it was poised over the top of the tank.

"Drop that or I'll bash you!" growled Alec, and Sidney dropped the stick like a hot potato. Then Alec's tone changed back to his usual reasonable voice. "Cobras ain't easy to feed. We just have to hope he'll eat proper and drink a lot. He needs fresh water every day. Who wants to fill up his drinking bowl from the stream?"

"Me!" yelled Sidney and, grabbing the bowl, he ran off.

Once Freddy was settled with food and water, Alec said to Tilly, "I've got to go back to the zoo for the late shift. Will you take Freddy back inside for the night? Make sure you wrap the sacks around the tank to keep him warm. I don't know how long I can keep him going without the heat they have in the reptile room."

"What will happen to him?" said Tilly.

"If he makes it to the weekend I might be able to find someone to take him. Fingers crossed, eh?" Then Alec screwed his peaked cap on his head and walked off, hands in his pockets, whistling.

Tilly called the children together and gave them all jobs to do. The little girls made sure the pets' boxes had clean grass, and the boy with the bow, who was called Miles, checked the tortoise's box. Rosy, keeping Tinkerbell carefully tucked under one arm, changed the parrot's water and filled up his bowl with seed. Pirate seemed to have taken to Rosy, and he tapped his beak on the cage when he saw her.

"Short rations," called out Tilly. "No idea where to get any more."

The two dogs, Bonny and Hanno, had relieved themselves outside. Tilly dug up some fresh earth and covered the number twos so no one would stand in it.

When she went back in the hut, she heard Rudi muttering to Hanno, "*Braver hund. Braver hund.*"

"I wonder what he's saying," she said to Rosy.

"I think I've worked it out," said Rosy, carefully closing the door to the parrot cage. "Braver is like bravo, well done. Hund is like hound, or dog, maybe. I think he's saying 'good dog'."

Tilly nodded and passed her hand across her brow. "I think we're ready for the night," she said, "but it's jolly hard work, and we have to do this every single day."

"We better tie the dogs up on short leads, well away from each other and the other pets," said Sidney. "Bonny this end and Hanno," he patted to a corner of the hut and nodded to Rudi, "'ere alright, mate?"

Rudi seemed to understand and with a nod said, "*Ja.*"

"Let's hope they all just go to sleep," said Tilly, as she pulled the door shut.

Bonny had already started to whine and Tilly had to resist the temptation to run inside for another cuddle. She didn't want everyone else doing the same or they would never get home for tea.

She went over to Rosy and said quietly, "It's getting late, and I just wanted to ask you about the zoo when we're evac—"

"—Oh, I almost forgot! The rules," cut in Rosy. She called out in her "Megan voice", "Right everyone, listen to me."

The children gathered round where Rosy and Tilly were standing.

Rudi wandered over to the thicket. He had what looked like a soldier's bugle slung over his back and now he took it off and held it in his hand. It had a big dent on the side.

He's keeping lookout, Tilly decided.

"We have to have some rules if this is going to work," said Rosy, taking a pencil from behind her ear and opening a notebook. "I've written a few down and we all have to abide by them."

"Who says?" called out Miles. He was quite chunky compared to the skinny Scudder boys and had already climbed most of the trees round the clearing.

"Tilly and me," said Rosy in a firm voice. "It's our den, we had it all summer and it was our idea to hide the pets."

Miles scowled, but he didn't say anything else.

"Rule 1," Rosy went on. "Don't all come at the same time every day. Otherwise grown-ups might spot us and get suspicious. Tilly and I will be here after breakfast. So the Scudders come at half past nine and..."

She continued around the circle until all the children were given an allotted time.

"What if we can't come? Who will feed Antony? He gets very hungry, Mummy says he's a growing rabbit," said Mary.

"Don't worry," said Tilly. "Me and Rosy will make sure all pets have food and water. Go on, Rosy."

"Rule 2: We take turns keeping lookout. If you see any grown-ups—"

"—or that snob on her horse," cut in Miles.

"—then you must whistle SOS. That's the signal to hide the pets in the den and then stand around the clearing looking as if we're just playing."

Rosy taught them all SOS and Sidney burped it out like thunderclaps.

"All right, well done everyone!" Rosy called out, calming them down. She consulted her notebook again.

"Rule 3: Everyone has to help clean out *all* the pets, not just their own, or it isn't fair.

"Rule 4: Everyone has to look out for each other's pets.

"Rule 5: Everyone *has* to bring some food. We're already very short."

Mary put her hand up. Rosy gave a sigh and nodded.

"What if you can't get any food? Antony likes carrots with the skin on." Tears rolled down her cheeks.

"She's such a cry-baby," Miles said with a sneer.

"Oh shut up, you idiot. Do you want to stay?" Tilly burst out.

"Course."

"Then jolly well behave yourself."

Pam put her hand up and Tilly rolled her eyes at Rosy.

"I can't remember all them rules," said the little girl in a tearful voice.

"We'll remind you," said Rosy, in a sharp voice. She stared at the notebook. "Rule 6: The emergency zoo is *our* secret. You can't tell anyone. I've invented a code so we can leave each other messages. It's like our password. You write the words backwards."

There were puzzled looks around the group and then Sidney cried out, "I get it."

He took a piece of chalk out of his pocket and wrote on the side of the hut:

sihT si eht ycnegremE ooZ

"I can't read that," whined Pam.

"Brilliant, Sid," said Rosy.

Sidney went bright red and scuffed his shoe on the ground.

"This... is... um... the—" started Miles.

"—Emergency Zoo!" finished Mary in triumph. "Ooh, I can't wait to write a code."

"If we 'ave codes and passwords, what are we called, zoo keepers?" muttered Neville.

"Mmm, not zoo keepers," said Rosy.

Tilly thought about Alec's snake. "How about The Cobras?"

"That's more like it," said Miles, his eyes lighting up. He stood up, raised his bow and shot an arrow towards the trees. "Now let the grown-ups try and kill our pets."

A cheer went up and, just as Tilly was going to shout at them to pipe down, the SOS sounded in low blasts.

Looking over her shoulder she could see Rudi blowing on his bugle, holding it with one hand, his head pointed upwards, Hanno tucked under his arm.

"Oh no!" cried out Rosy. "Grown-up alert, everyone!"

But it wasn't grown-ups who pushed through the thicket and into the clearing. Tilly recognized both of them. Her heart sank to her boots.

Chapter 9

EXTREME DANGER

Wednesday late afternoon, 30th August 1939

Conor arrived first in the clearing. He was a tall, broad-shouldered lad, with black hair falling over his forehead, and large square hands which clenched into fists as hard as iron.

But even worse – he had a huge boxer dog with him, straining on the end of a chain. Behind Conor was Bill, his horrid sidekick. Bill was thin and pasty faced, a sly boy, but only a year older than Tilly. Conor was fourteen and much bigger than the boys in the zoo.

Before she could say anything, Conor snarled, "Get him, Boxer!"

The dog leapt forward, opened his enormous jaws – the size of a crocodile, thought Tilly – and closed his teeth around Rudi's thin, white leg. Rudi dropped his bugle and screamed.

Tilly stared in horror, her mind a jumble of thoughts. I have to do something, anything, she told herself. This is war and I have to be brave but her knees were shaking.

"Call your dog off," she cried out to Conor, as Rudi's screams grew louder. She took a step forward. "Rudi's only nine."

"Rudi? That ain't English – what do you think, mate?" called out Conor.

"Nah, sounds enemy to me," said Bill and he spat on the ground.

"What you girlies doing out here with an enemy-kid? What's he doing with that bugle – sending a signal to German spies?" said Conor.

Bill snorted. He had shaggy, pale blond hair and a nervous twitch around his mouth.

Stupid creep, thought Tilly.

"Who're you calling a girl?" said Miles, beginning to latch an arrow into his bow.

"You're *all* girls," sneered Conor. "Playing out here in the woods with the enemy and your lousy pets. You need a real dog like my Boxer." He gave a high-pitched whistle and Boxer let go of Rudi's leg. He scuttled away into the den.

Rosy took a step forward and said in her best Megan voice, "What do you want? We're just playing out and I would've thought you were a bit old for our games."

Sniggers went up around the children.

"We was just passing," said Conor. "Anyways, this is a bit of a rum place to keep your pets."

"We're saving 'em from being died, so you shut up!" shouted Pam.

That's torn it, thought Tilly. She's given us away.

"Who'd want to keep your mangy mutts alive, anyway?" said Conor with a snort.

"You have a pet too. Don't you care about him?" said Tilly. "He looks thirsty to me."

Boxer was sitting up, drool pouring down the side of his mouth as he panted, tongue hanging out. To Tilly's surprise, Conor dropped to his knee beside his dog and, stroking his head gently, he murmured, "All right, boy? We'll get you some water, eh?"

Bill looked around, scuffing his boot in the earth, hands in his pockets, as if he didn't know what to do when Conor wasn't hurling insults around.

Then Conor straightened and said in a gruff voice, "Boxers need a lot to drink. You got any water?"

He stared at Tilly and Tilly stared back, arms folded. But maybe he does care about his pet, she thought.

"You can take him to the stream in the wood," Rosy said. "Then we'd very much like you to go away and not come back."

"You ain't gonna let her talk like that, Conor," snarled Bill. Then he turned on Tilly and said, "You lot better watch out or we'll tell everyone where your stupid dogs are. Maybe we'll come back and let them out, right, mate?"

"Right," said Conor but he was staring at his dog with concern on his face.

Tilly stuck her chin in the air and said, "Just you try and you'll see what you get."

An arrow whizzed past and landed in front of Boxer.

Conor stumbled backwards, his face creased with anger. He pulled the arrow up and said, "You trying to kill my dog? No one touches him. You hear me!" His face had gone very red and then he brandished the arrow at Miles and said, "You need a right bashing!"

Miles stood his ground, bow drawn, ready to load a second arrow. "You and whose army?" he jeered.

But Tilly could see his ears had gone very red.

Then, without any warning, Conor threw Boxer's chain at Bill and launched himself at Miles. Boxer lunged after him, nearly pulling Bill over.

Conor punched Miles on the nose and blood spurted out. Miles gave a yell and kicked out at Conor, stopping him for a few seconds.

It's going to be all right, Tilly told herself. Miles is no pushover.

But Conor was older and much stronger. He punched Miles in the mouth and then pulled his hair hard. Miles screamed out.

"You fight dirty!" shouted Neville.

"I'll knock his block off!" yelled Sidney, but Neville grabbed him and held him back.

"Let me go, I'll kill 'im." Sidney struggled in Neville's arms, his fists punching at the air.

Conor let out a roar and punched Miles hard in the stomach. Miles crumpled to the ground and Conor stood over him, hands on his hips like a prize fighter, grinning.

CHAPTER 9

"You filthy coward!" screamed Tilly.

Bill lost the battle to hold Boxer and the great dog leapt towards Miles, growling. Miles squealed and rolled up into a ball, his arms over his head.

"Call him off, you pigs!" shouted Rosy. "If the Germans invade, you can fight them. Why are you going to war with us?"

Rudi had come to the doorway of the hut and Conor nodded towards him, "Your mate, the enemy-kid. He's not one of us. You'd better keep *him* on a lead." He grabbed Boxer's chain and called to Bill, "Come on, let's move out."

The boys slouched off in the direction of the stream.

Rosy was down on her knees, her handkerchief turning a bright red as she pressed it against Miles's battered nose. "You were so brave, you deserve a medal."

"I'm not scared of them bullies," declared Miles, but Tilly knew he was. They all were.

The lovely afternoon at the hut had been spoilt and everyone started to pick up their bikes. Then Rosy called out, "Wait a minute. I think we should take an oath."

"What loaf?" asked Pam.

"*Oath*, stupid!" said Sidney. "It means you swear to keep something secret, right, Nev?"

Neville nodded.

"Good idea," said Tilly. "I swear on Bonny's life I will never give away the Emergency Zoo."

"I swear on Clover's death," said Pam.

One by one all the children swore and then Rosy cried, "*Doof Tep* Cobras!"

"*Doof tep, doof tep,*" shouted the children.

They drifted away, Rudi jogging off behind the Scudders, the bugle bumping away on his back.

Miles gathered his arrows and bow, and when they were finally alone, he said to Rosy and Tilly, "What if they come back tonight and try to let the pets out? I think one of us should keep watch."

"I was thinking the same," said Tilly.

"But your Dad would never let you sleep out in the woods, and I can't imagine even mentioning such a thing to Megan," said Rosy.

"We don't tell them," said Tilly.

Rosy stared at her, eyes wide. "What do you mean?"

"Simple. I say that you want me to camp in your garden tonight and you tell Megan the same, only at my house."

"But what if they speak to each other?" said Rosy, in her anxious voice.

"It's a chance we'll have to take. We live three streets apart – they don't bump into each other that often." Rosy still looked uncertain so Tilly said, "Look, if Conor and Bill come back tonight, they might do something really stupid. I don't know what I'd do if they let Bonny escape."

"I'll come too," said Miles. "I don't know what it's like round yours but all my Mum and Dad do is argue about the war, dig up the garden and listen to the radio. I'll tell them Scout Leader wants us to practise camping before the war starts."

"And I'll say that we're going to sleep out in the garden in a tent a friend's lending us, so we have an excuse to bring a blanket," said Rosy in an excited voice. "That'll work."

"And food," said Miles. "We got to have food – biscuits and stuff. We'll have a smashing night and make sure those nincompoops stay away."

Tilly and Rosy laughed at the word nincompoops and they all felt much better.

"Meet back here after tea," said Tilly.

They all picked up their bikes, pushed through the thicket and set off across the fields, the girls side by side, with Miles weaving in and out around them. The sun was still quite high in the sky and larks were calling in the warm air over their heads. Bright red poppies bobbed in between the tall ears of yellow corn, and Tilly felt she could cycle for ever in the sunshine.

They crossed the canal and parted at the corner, but then she found herself stuck behind a huge lorry.

"Here it comes," called out Mrs Benson, who was leaning over her garden gate.

"What is it?" Tilly called back.

"We're getting our own anti-aircraft gun in the park."

Tilly mounted the pavement and cycled round the side of the lorry, which had halted for a moment. Now she could see it was an army lorry, painted in khaki, and, loaded onto its open flat bottom, was a huge gun with wheels bigger than a tractor and a barrel which reached up into the sky, pointing straight at the sun. She felt tiny as an ant as she stared up at it.

"That'll blow them Nazis out of the sky," said the man next door as he walked past, pushing his cap back on his head.

But if we need a gun that big, thought Tilly, how big are the bombs the Germans are going to drop? Shuddering despite the warm sun, she rode up to her front gate. The Anderson shelter in their back garden seemed ridiculously flimsy beside the massive gun and the even more massive threat of bombers in the sky. The war was marching ever closer, booming in their ears, threatening the houses and the gardens, the schools and the people and all the animals in all the countries in the world. Nothing was going to prevent it, however much they wished it would just go away.

Chapter 10

ONCE WAR BREAKS OUT...

Wednesday evening, 30th August 1939

"You can't go *camping* at a time like this, Matilda," said Mum as they finished tea. "Germany's threatening to invade Poland and we don't know when it might start up here. What if you're in a tent and the bombs start falling or we're all gassed? What do you say, Dad?" Her mother frowned and clattered plates together.

Tilly's head dropped. If Mum wasn't on her side then Dad certainly wouldn't be.

But Dad said, "I think it's a very good idea."

"You do?" said Tilly, her head jerking upwards.

"It'll help to toughen you up a bit with the war coming. But only one night, mind, and don't go making work for Donald and Megan. The grown-ups have enough to do. Time for the news, Mother."

CHAPTER 10

It was six o'clock and, as usual, a tense silence fell over the household. They went into the sitting room and sat down. Outside the open window nothing stirred, as if the whole neighbourhood, even the birds, were listening and waiting for the news no one wanted to hear.

"*This is London*," boomed out the solemn tones of the newsreader, as the final chimes of Big Ben echoed round the house.

Tilly sat cross-legged on the floor and flicked through a comic, only half listening while the newsreader droned on about Hitler and the British navy mobilizing.

"*...but Poland remains in grave danger... the Prime Minister is going to Buckingham Palace for talks with the King this evening... the government has sent another message to Herr Hitler to try to avert war...*"

Then there came the words that made Tilly's blood run cold.

"*...and the government has made it clear that no pets will be allowed in public air raid shelters once war breaks out...*"

Tilly felt her throat close up and a shudder went through her. A picture of loud bangs and everyone running in the streets came into her mind. She would be carrying Bonny and as she arrived at the door to the public shelter, Ted Bow would block the way, rifle ready, saying, "No pets in here, love; best shoot her, it's the kindest thing to do."

"Tilly? Whatever's the matter with you?" her mother said, frowning as Dad switched off the radio.

Tilly let out a loud sob and said, "Poor Bonny – even if she finds a shelter they won't let her inside." It wasn't difficult to let a couple of tears fall, and Mum reached down and patted her knee.

"Well, that's what the government's decided," said Dad, looking over at Tilly as she sat on the carpet. "They're setting up the anti-aircraft battery in the park and I saw a barrage balloon go up this evening beyond the factory. Speaking of which," his voice deepened and Tilly's head jerked up, "what's this I hear about kids hiding their pets near the canal in those old factories? The neighbours were talking about it. What do you know about that, Tilly?"

Tilly looked down at her comic, chills running up and down her spine. Has someone given us away already? "I haven't heard anything, but I'll keep an ear out," she murmured and then she blew her nose very loudly on her handkerchief.

Dad gave a bit of a snort, but he went out of the room, which was a relief.

"You didn't eat very much at tea," said Mum.

"No… I… I'm not very hungry tonight."

"I hope you're not going down with something," said her mother, feeling her forehead.

"No, honest, Mum, I'm fine. I'm just so sad without my darling Bonny."

"Well, perhaps it was for the best she ran off. She can forage for herself, can't she?" said Mum, in a soothing voice.

Tilly gave a little nod, wiping her eyes with the handkerchief.

"Now now," went on Mum, "I thought I'd make you some sandwiches to take over to Rosy's in case you're hungry later. I don't want you bothering Megan."

"Thanks ever so much, Mum. That would be lovely."

Tilly walked carefully from the room and, once out of sight, raced upstairs, her heart thumping. That was a close shave, she told herself.

She couldn't wait to see Bonny now, and feel her rough tongue licking her face and smell her musty, doggy smell. She rolled up her torch in her blanket and pulled on an extra jumper and a second pair of socks.

Then she ran downstairs again, calling out, "I'm ready."

Mum came into the hallway holding a large paper bag of food. "There's enough to share – we don't want Rosy's family to say we're mean. Gumboots, mac, and take a warm scarf, please, Matilda. The late-night air will turn cold."

"I'll be warm as toast," said Tilly.

"I could come over and make sure the tent won't leak or fall down or anything," said Dad, leaning in the doorway of the sitting room, his face more relaxed.

It reminded Tilly with a pang what fun they used to have before all this talk of war. Dad liked nothing better than taking her and Mum for long walks down the canal, finding a corner to have a picnic, and he always lit a small fire. Tilly would toast the bread from her sandwiches, and sometimes they stayed out until dark. All that was over now the war was coming, and the grown-ups were so short tempered and worried all the time.

She stared up at Dad's big brown eyes, crinkled round the edges as he grinned down at her, wanting to join in with the fun. She hated to disappoint him. But she said, "Oh, no need, Dad. Donald's dying to do all that."

Dad gave a shrug as if he didn't care, but she could see that he did. She kissed them both goodbye, went out of the front door, grabbed her bike and set off towards Rosy's house.

It was still warm and sunny outside, and she couldn't help feeling on the edge of a great adventure. They were going to sleep outdoors for the very first time in their lives, without any grown-ups, and, like soldiers in a war, they were going to guard their pets.

She glanced over her shoulder to check Mum and Dad were safely inside and then she turned her bike back down the street and towards the canal. Now's a good time to talk about the zoo when we get evacuated, Tilly told herself. I think I've got a jolly good plan. I hope Rosy agrees.

Up ahead she saw Rosy on the bridge and called out, "Hi there!"

As she cycled up alongside Rosy, Tilly blurted out the words she'd been holding in all day. "What are we going to do about the zoo when we're evacuated? Do you think we should ask Alec to take over? He's too young to be called up and too old to be evacuated, I think. So he could do it, couldn't he?"

"Goodness, I haven't really thought about it. Yes, I suppose so, what do you think?"

"I'm not sure, but we have to think of something, we go next Tuesday."

They cycled along for a few moments, both deep in thought, and then Tilly called over her shoulder, "Oh blow it! Let's forget about it for tonight."

"That's the spirit," said Rosy. "Come on then."

They stood up on their pedals and rode over the bumpy ground of the fields until they reached the thicket. Pushing through the brambles, they went into the clearing and dropped their bikes on the grass. Tilly could hear Bonny's joyful barking before she got to the door, and then all the animals started mewing and barking, squawking and squealing.

Hanno had started to yap loudly and Pirate seemed to squawk back at him, as though they were having a proper conversation.

"Do you think Pirate speaks German?" said Tilly as she bent down to release Bonny.

"Possibly," said Rosy. "Parrots are very intelligent. He almost said Hello to me yesterday, but I'm not sure we're feeding him properly, so maybe he can't speak if he's hungry."

She lifted Tinkerbell out of her crate and smoothed down the fur around her ears. "Oh look, Tinks just opened her eye a bit. I think she's looking better today – what do you think?"

Tilly glanced over at Tinkerbell and said, "Oh yes." Even though she really wasn't sure. Tinkerbell hadn't been well for a couple of days. Hopefully she'd get better soon, before they made a plan for the future of the zoo.

Bonny ran outside and Tilly followed, enjoying the cool evening air on her bare legs. Gnats buzzed around her head and a bee settled on an open flower in a last ray of light. "If the bombs fall on our street, Bonny," she said aloud, "I'll bring Mum and Dad to the den to sleep with the emergency zoo. Then they'll be pleased that the children decided to save the pets, won't they?"

As if she understood every word, Bonny raised her head and fixed her liquid brown eyes on Tilly. They stood together quietly for a moment.

Already the woods were settling down for the night. Pools of black were spreading under the trees, but somehow hiding away from the grown-ups made Tilly feel safe. The whole summer, with its boiling hot weather, crazy thunderstorms and now the calm sunny days, had been so ominous with war creeping closer and closer. Maybe if they had taken more notice sooner, they could have made a proper plan for all the animals. But all Tilly had wanted to do was play in their lovely den. The last few days with all the worries and responsibility for so many pets had taken some of the fun away.

But now, with a whole delicious night to look forward to, she felt the worries fall from her shoulders.

"We're going to have such fun, Bonny Bonbons. Come on!"

Bonny gave a high-pitched yap and they ran together back to the hut where Miles was piling wood for a campfire.

"Brought some potatoes, we can roast 'em," said Miles, nudging a bulging sack with his toe. "We'll havc a feast."

"A midnight feast, Tinkerbell," Rosy said, as she sat cross-legged on the ground with her little cat.

This night belongs to the children, Tilly told herself, with a happy sigh.

Chapter 11

NO EYES... NO NOSE... NO MOUTH...

Wednesday night, 30th August 1939

By the time it was properly dark, the children had made up their beds in the hut. Tilly and Rosy were next to each other and Miles was further away behind the wall at the end. Miles had worked hard to build up a roaring fire, and the potatoes were tucked into the bottom in the hottest part.

"They take ages," he said, poking them with a long stick, "but nothing tastes better. I got some butter too."

Rosy had brought some meat scraps for the dogs and the parrot.

Tilly had some carrots for the rabbits. She opened Antony's crate, calling out, "Here you are, my darling, I've sliced up some juicy carrot for you."

Toffee and Apple were making wheeking sounds and snuffling through the hay.

"They sound very hungry," she said, as the sounds got louder. She started to untie the string holding the chicken-wire in place.

Miles came over and pulled an apple out of his pocket. Taking out his scout knife, he sliced the apple into pieces, dropping them into the cage. He threw the core away and said, "That should do it."

The guinea pigs were soon munching away happily and Tilly was amazed at how relieved she was. The responsibility for feeding their entire emergency zoo felt almost too much at times.

Miles had saved a piece of apple for Domino. Tilly watched, fascinated, as the rat sat up in Miles's cupped hands and, holding the fruit between his paws, delicately nibbled away until it was all gone.

"He eats as politely as Tinkerbell."

"Rats are very misunderstood," said Miles, dropping Domino back in the top pocket of his shirt. "They're really very clean and they're enormously clever."

He went off to check on the fire, and Tilly said in a quiet voice to Rosy, "Do you think Megan or Donald are suspicious about the zoo? Dad practically interrogated me at teatime about rumours of kids hiding pets near the canal."

CHAPTER 11

Rosy was poking a piece of fat through the bars of the parrot's cage. Pirate gave a squawk and leaned forward. Tilly was sure he would peck off Rosy's fingers but instead he just pulled the fat away and let it drop to the floor of the cage. Then he jumped down from his perch and started to peck away. He must be very hungry, she thought. Makes him even more bad tempered.

"They haven't said anything," said Rosy. "Megan's so much stricter than Mummy ever was. It's ridiculous. We had terrible rows when I first went to live with them. I thought she'd send me away, but Donald's nice—"

"Yes, he is," agreed Tilly.

"—and he's always saying what a good person Megan is, which I know is true, and I'm very grateful she looks after me – otherwise I'd be in an orphanage."

They both shuddered at the thought.

"But she doesn't really *know* me, Tilly," Rosy went on, her voice rising as she spoke. "Not like *you* do. She never reads books, and she's not at all interested in pets or finding out about anything. Daddy and me went to the library every week. Daddy loved books as much as me."

Rosy fell silent and Tilly squeezed her arm to show she understood how much her friend was missing her parents.

It must be so awful, Tilly thought. She just couldn't imagine Mum and Dad not being there, even though they annoyed her ever such a lot sometimes.

The two girls stood staring into each other's eyes, their faces white in the light from the torch, and then Rosy turned away, wiping a tear from her eye. "I've got some buns," she said in a small voice. "I'll take them outside for our feast."

Tilly watched her go as she shook out the scraps bag, letting Bonny lick up the last titbits. Then she peered into the crates, shining her torch through the chicken-wire. The small pets seemed to be asleep. But they would need more food again tomorrow, and the next day, and every day after that.

Outside, the fire was roaring away, sending bright orange flames into the dark night. Tilly laid out the bag of cheese and pickle sandwiches on a blanket spread on the ground. Rosy's buns were already there, and Miles had added butter and a few apples.

Rosy was sitting on her mac, Tinkerbell wrapped up tight in the pink flannel, asleep in her lap. "Dear little Tinks," Rosy was whispering. "You have a good sleep and, when you're better, we'll have some fun. I'll let you chase all the birds in the woods, I promise."

Tilly laid out her mac too and sat down, wrapping her scarf around her neck and pulling Bonny's warm body onto her legs. The night air was getting chilly, but Bonny didn't seem to mind. She lay with her head tucked in, eyes blinking at the campfire. *She's happy to be with me*, Tilly told herself, enjoying the feel of the thick fur through her fingers. *Me and Bonny know each other inside out – we'll always love each other.*

Miles had taken his rat out of his pocket and let it run from hand to hand. It was as white as Mary's rabbit, with a long grey tail and whiskers, which never stopped quivering.

"Surely your parents don't care about your rat," Tilly said. "He can't exactly eat very much."

"Mum hates Domino," said Miles with a grin. "She's delighted that she's got an excuse now to get rid of him, even though it means war. She thinks he's escaped from his cage but I keep him in a little box under my bed. I'm going to train him to spot German spies. He'll be good at that – won't you, Domino, boy?" He put his nose on the tip of the rat's quivering nose.

Tilly gave a sarcastic snort. "Well, the Germans must be quaking in their boots."

They all laughed and then Rosy said, "Let's play pictures in the fire. We take it in turns to say what we can see, like a fairy-tale castle and a dragon fighting a prince."

"Nah," said Miles, leaning forward, his face glowing red in the light from the flames. "We should tell ghost stories. That's what we do at camp. Scout Leader tells the best ones. I'll start."

He looks like a small devil, thought Tilly, and a chill fluttered down her spine.

Miles had a scout knife in a sheath hooked onto his belt. He took it out now and began to whittle away at a bit of wood, as he told his story. "There was this man walking home and he had to take a short cut through a graveyard. It was a very dark night and it was raining, and he heard a horse and cart come up behind him."

"In a graveyard? How stupid," said Rosy, stroking Tinkerbell's fluffy ear.

"You're stupid," said Miles. "How else can they take dead people in their coffins to their graves? You ever lifted a coffin?"

"Hardly," said Rosy, in her Megan voice.

Tilly snickered and said, "Go on, anyway."

"So the man stops and waits for the cart and calls up, Can you give me a lift?" said Miles, making his voice as ghostly as possible. "The cart driver has a big cloak on with the hood up against the rain, but he nods, so the man gets on and they go off. The man starts to tell the driver a story he's heard from the village people – that the graveyard's haunted."

Miles stopped and made ghostly noises, which sounded more like a frog with a cough, thought Tilly. She threw an acorn at him and the girls laughed.

Then Rosy said, "Shush… listen… what's that?"

They fell silent. At first, all they could hear was a rustling between the trees – like a small animal or bird snuffling around – and then, clear as a bell, from the direction of the stream in the woods, came the hooting of an owl. It stopped and then started again.

"My first real owl," said Rosy, in a hushed voice.

"I wish we could stay here for ever," said Miles. "My school's being evacuated on Tuesday and my partner's Steven Fuller. He's a complete nincompoop."

Tilly and Rosy fell about laughing at that word again, and then Miles said, in a huff, "Shall I finish the story or not?"

"Oh go on," said Tilly. "Might as well."

"Well, the cart driver doesn't speak, and the man goes on about how the villagers have seen a tall figure walking round the graveyard at night – a figure with no face."

"What do you mean, no face?" said Tilly.

Miles's eyes narrowed as he leaned towards them, his face glowing blood red in the firelight, and hissed, "No eyes, no nose, no mouth, no hair, just dead white… skin!"

Rosy gasped and shot Tilly a look, and then Miles said, "What do you think the cart driver said?"

"What?" whispered Tilly.

Miles gave a creepy laugh and said, "The driver turned to the man, lifted his hood and said, 'You mean, like me!'"

He broke into a cackling scream and bashed the fire until the air glowed with sparks.

Tilly's hand flew to her mouth and Rosy bent over Tinkerbell.

Then a roar went up behind them, and a crashing came through the undergrowth.

Oh God! The faceless man's coming, thought Tilly in terror.

But it was Neville thundering towards them, with Sidney close behind. They tore up to the fire, leapt off their bikes and let them drop onto the grass.

"Got any food, Tilly?" panted Sidney. "I'm starving."

Tilly let out a laugh of relief and said, "What on earth are you doing here? What did you tell your parents? You'd better not have given the emergency zoo away."

"Course not, keep your 'air on," growled Neville. "Me Dad's working nights and Mum's asleep with the baby and Pam. They don't know nothing about it and we ain't gonna tell 'em, eh Sid?"

"You can trust us," said Sidney, who was already rummaging through the packages on the blanket. "Cor blimey! Cheese sandwiches."

He leant back on his knees, his thin face turned up towards Tilly, and she could see the hunger raging in his eyes.

"Didn't you have any tea?" she said.

"We ain't 'ad nothing 'cept a slice of bread and marge this morning," said Sidney.

Neville shoved him so hard he nearly fell in the fire. "What you telling them that for? Ain't no one's business, like Dad says."

Neville's face had gone red with shame, and he pretended to rummage in his pocket for something, but Tilly could see it was full of holes and there was nothing there.

"The food's for sharing," said Rosy, saving the day with her Megan voice.

Tilly handed round the sandwiches. There was enough for one each and one left over, which she quietly gave to Sidney. He took it, tore it in half and gave one piece to his brother. Neville hesitated, and then, still looking down, took it and stuffed it into his mouth. After that, Tilly gave everyone two apples and a bun each.

"Doesn't everything taste wonderful outside?" said Rosy, and they all grunted with agreement, mouths full.

"But I'm still 'ungry," moaned Sidney, clutching his stomach and rolling around on the grass.

"That was just the first course," said Tilly. "We've got potatoes roasting in the fire. Are they ready yet, Miles?"

Sidney gave a loud whoop and threw himself to his feet. Spreading out his arms, he turned into a fighter plane, racing round the fire, rat-tat-tatting like a machine gun.

Miles pulled a potato out of the ashes and sliced it open with his knife. "Perfect," he pronounced, and rolled the rest out onto the grass. He sliced potatoes for everyone, dropping knobs of butter into the centre. The children burnt their mouths and hands as they ate, stopping only to gasp how delicious they were.

"This is the best dinner I ever 'ad," pronounced Sidney, his chin dripping butter and his mouth black from the charred potato skins.

When the food had gone and the fire began to die down, Neville said, "Any sign of Conor and Bill?"

"No fear," said Miles. "We'll give 'em what for if they come round here."

"Me and Nev reckoned you needed some more men," said Sidney.

"Thank you very much," said Rosy in her Megan voice. "After all, me and Tilly are *only* girls."

Tilly snorted and they rolled their eyes at each other.

The boys ducked their heads and Miles threw some more twigs on the fire. It flared up and Tilly put out her hands. She shivered a little, and for a moment thought of her warm bed at home and Mum and Dad murmuring in the living room below her bedroom.

Rosy said, as if reading her thoughts, "Why don't we put out the fire and all go to bed."

Sidney gave a yawn and went over to Neville's bike. He pulled out a couple of sacks from the basket. "Len next door give 'em to us. Says they keep 'im right warm when 'e goes fruit picking in Kent. They sleep out in the orchards."

They all went inside. Sidney and Neville lay down under their sacks next to Miles's blanket, in "the boys' room", as Rosy dubbed it.

Tilly pulled Bonny over to her blanket and, for the first time that week, settled down to sleep with Bonny's soft, warm body across her legs, just like at home. Rosy made a cushion out of her coat and laid the sleeping Tinkerbell next to her, kissing the soft fur behind her ear.

"This has been the best night of my life," she whispered to Tilly.

"Absolutely," said Tilly. "I don't want to go home."

"Me neither."

Pirate gave a sleepy squawk of agreement and Hanno seemed to yap back in his dreams. Bonny changed positions on Tilly's legs a couple of times, making herself properly comfortable. There was an earthy, musty smell in the shed – partly from the caged animals and partly from the crumbling walls and mud floor. Tilly snuggled under her blanket, feeling very cosy now that she could have Bonny on her bed again. There were all sorts of tiny noises coming from the small pets in the cages.

Miles called out, "Two points if you guess which animal from the sounds."

"You're on," called back Tilly and Rosy together, and then they both giggled.

"Quiet!"

Tilly held her breath, and in the silence they could hear snuffling.

"Guinea pig," said Sidney.

"Got to say the name."

"Don't know their blimmin' names."

"That's Toffee," said Rosy.

"Two points to the girls!" cried out Tilly, and shouts of "Not fair!" came from the boys' corner.

"Do snakes make any noise?" whispered Tilly to Rosy.

"No."

Pirate gave a loud squawk.

"Pirate!" yelled Sidney. "Two points."

They were quiet for a couple of minutes, and then Hanno gave a yap and Pirate squawked back.

Like lightning, Rosy said in her clear voice, "That's Hanno followed by Pirate, four points. The girls win!"

More shouts and jeers from the boys' corner and then everyone seemed to agree that it was time to fall asleep.

Tilly could feel her eyes closing. She was sure all the boys were asleep, and at least one of them was snoring. "I never imagined I would spend the night in a zoo," she whispered to Rosy. "What totally amazing fun!"

"I wish we could stay here for ever and let the grown-ups have their stupid war a long way away."

"Agreed."

They slipped off to sleep with the sound of the owl hooting in the wood.

In her dreams, Tilly was walking with Bonny to the hut. She could smell smoke and she told Bonny that Sidney was cooking a big dinner for everyone. When Tilly looked down, the little dog had no eyes.

Then a blood-curdling scream split the air.

"It's the man with no face," screamed Tilly, fully awake now, and Rosy sat bolt upright, Tinkerbell in her arms.

Chapter 12

OUR FIRST FALLEN SOLDIER

Before dawn, Thursday 31st August 1939

Tilly threw back her blanket and grabbed Bonny, who was yelping and whining. Weird, ghostly sounds were coming from all round the hut.

The boys were awake now, and Miles said in a loud whisper, "We'd better see what's out there, hadn't we?"

But no one moved, and then something hit the side of the hut with a great crash, and dust and cobwebs fell from the ceiling.

Hanno and Bonny started barking and whining, and Rosy screamed and leapt to her feet, running forward.

"Come back!" shrieked Tilly, almost choking on the dust.

Rosy hesitated at the door, and for a moment there was a silence.

Then a high-pitched contorted voice said, "We're coming to get you."

"It's that idiot, Conor!" yelled Sidney, and he ran to the door, wrenched it open and yelled, "Come over here, you mongrels!"

Inside the hut there was bedlam. Pirate was squawking and patrolling up and down his perch frantically, the little pets were squealing in their straw, Hanno and Bonny were whining and barking and Tilly suddenly thought – what if they break in and set Freddy free? Then we'll be in such trouble, letting a poisonous snake out.

Releasing Bonny from her lead, she marched out of the den, drew herself up to her full height and cried out, "Stop it right now, you lot, or Bonny will get you!"

Bonny had started to growl and she sounded quite menacing. It was only just beginning to get light and the trees were casting deep pools of black all round the clearing. Squinting in the gloom, Tilly could just make out Conor with Boxer and Billy. They were clutching themselves with laughter.

"Ain't you got no sense of humour?" sneered Conor and he patted Boxer's head, murmuring, "Good boy, good dog."

"Oh for goodness' sakes," said Rosy, in her Megan voice. She had tucked her hair behind her ears and was smoothing down her skirt in an effort to look presentable. "Why don't you just leave us alone, unless what you really want is to play with us and all our pets."

"You must be joking," said Conor. It was getting lighter now, and Tilly could see his dark hair flopping in his eyes and the line of his mouth as he threw them a mocking grin. "Can't help it if you don't know how to keep *your* pets safe in the war."

"Are you that stupid?" called out Sidney, and even Tilly was surprised.

Conor gave him a wary look and pulled Boxer closer. He really does care about his dog, she thought. If only he wasn't such a bully – he could be quite useful. There was something about Conor which she had noticed before. As though he wasn't as tough as he wanted everyone to think; but there was no time to worry about that now. He was putting the whole zoo at risk by behaving so stupidly.

"'Ow long do you think your dog's gonna live, Conor?" Sidney went on.

"Don't know what you mean."

"Ain't you seen the queues outside the vet? They're killing 'undreds of pets. Me and me brother saw the bonfires down by the canal last night."

"What bonfires?" asked Rosy.

"To burn the bodies," muttered Neville. "They threw some of 'em in the canal in sacks, weighted down to make 'em sink. But there's too many. They got dogs, cats, parrots, all sorts, burning away like mad."

Rosy gasped.

"That's what's going to 'appen to Boxer, ain't it?" said Sidney, and he spat on the ground.

"Don't listen to those dumbos," said Bill.

But Conor looked as though all the fight had gone out of him as he fondled Boxer's ears. "Come on," he growled at Bill and, pulling on Boxer's chain, he strode away.

"Good riddance to bad rubbish," muttered Tilly, but she wasn't sure if she really meant it.

Miles gave a laugh and said, "We just won our first battle, eh, Cobras?"

Sidney leapt in the air, whooping, and took off round the clearing, arms out like a fighter plane again.

CHAPTER 12

It must be properly morning, Tilly decided. The sun was climbing above the trees and the woods were light and airy in the early morning air. She called Bonny and they went down to the stream – Bonny for a drink, and Tilly to rinse her face.

As they walked back to the hut, Tilly called out, "Any food left? I'm starving."

She could see Miles and Neville leaning in the doorway, and Sidney was sitting cross-legged on the grass, his head in his hands.

"Did you check on the pets?" she asked Neville.

He didn't reply, but nodded into the hut. Then Tilly heard sobbing and, going inside, she saw Rosy huddled on the ground, a limp fur bundle in her arms and tears pouring down her face.

"Rosy, what is it?" said Tilly. A blade of fear sliced through her.

"Tinkerbell's died," sobbed Rosy.

"Let me see. How do you know? Maybe she's just sound asleep." Tilly put her hand out but Rosy pulled away.

Neville said in a quiet voice, "Ain't no use, Tills. Me and Sidney see dead rats all the time in the yard. She's proper gone."

Tilly dropped down on the floor of the hut and patted Rosy's arm.

"She must have gone when I was asleep," said Rosy, through her tears. "I didn't know she was so ill. I abandoned her—"

"—No you didn't!" cut in Tilly, horrified.

For a moment, she couldn't say anything else. Her best friend had just lost her darling pet, her last link back to her parents and the happy life before they passed away. This was a complete disaster. She cast about for something to say. "There was nothing anyone could have done, Rose, is there? I mean look, you came here to sleep with her last night. That's not abandoning, is it? Dear little Tinkerbell knew… she knew… well, how much you absolutely loved her."

"But you can't be sure."

"I am. I completely and utterly am."

They fell silent and Rosy started to smooth the matted fur from around Tinkerbell's mouth, which was tightly closed.

Tilly reached out and gently stroked the cat's paw but she could feel how stiff it was and, after a few seconds, she let her hand drop back in her lap.

All around the hut she could hear the sounds of the pets waking up and foraging around in their crates for bits of food. One of the rabbits was thumping against the wooden wall, making a hollow echoing sound. Bonny and Hanno were both lying on their bellies, noses on their paws, looking as miserable as Tilly felt – but that was probably because they were hungry. All the pets needed food and water, but the boys were just standing around with their hands in their pockets, and the clock was ticking.

If we don't go back soon, thought Tilly, *then the grown-ups will know we told them a pack of lies about camping in each other's gardens, and they might stop us going out for days. What will happen to the pets? I've got to do something.*

Then the perfect plan came to her.

"A funeral," she said and Rosy paused in her sobbing. "We'll bury Tinkerbell here by the hut so that she will always be a part of the emergency zoo."

"We have to put her name," said Rosy in a tiny voice. "I don't want her forgotten, not ever. Like I never forget Mummy and Daddy."

"Of course," said Tilly.

"We'll bury 'er with full military 'onours," said Neville.

"That's right," put in Miles in a quiet voice. "Tinkerbell is our first fallen soldier, and we got to do it properly."

"And we have to do it before our parents expect us home for breakfast," muttered Tilly.

It was already eight o'clock, and if they left it much longer, the grown-ups would catch them out.

Sidney came into the hut and started to root around in a corner. "'Ere," he said, brandishing an old tin box. "Put 'er in that, keep 'er safe from the foxes."

Before Rosy could sob about Tinkerbell being eaten by a fox, Tilly said in a bright voice, "Oh that's lovely, Sidney, well done – and it's got a good, strong lid. You can fill it with moss and stuff, Rose."

"And her favourite bit of pink flannel," said Rosy, wiping her eyes with the back of her sleeve.

"Come on, boys," said Miles, brandishing his knife. "Let's go and find a good, safe spot and start digging."

The boys disappeared and Tilly cradled Tinkerbell while Rosy prepared her final resting place. She murmured to Tinkerbell while she worked, "So you see, my darling little cat, you'll be perfectly safe in here, and very cosy, and I'll come every day and put flowers on your grave like me and Megan and Donald do for Mummy and Daddy every Sunday after church."

Tears welled up in Tilly's eyes and she fought to keep them back. I mustn't cry in front of Rosy, she told herself, but it was so hard not to sob out loud.

Rosy took Tinkerbell and laid her tenderly in the box.

Sidney came back and said, "We got a smashin' place for 'er, come and see." They all went round to a sunny spot at the back of the hut. Miles and Neville were scrabbling in a hole almost two feet deep and wide enough to take the box.

"Gotta make it deep," puffed Neville. "Keep 'er safe."

Tilly helped Rosy make a small cross with some string and two nice straight branches which Miles cut from a tree.

"I'll make a special sign with her name when I get home," said Rosy in a low voice. "I can use the oil paints Donald gave me for my birthday. The rain won't wash it away then."

"Good idea," said Tilly.

They all stood around the grave while Rosy lowered the box inside. The boys pushed the earth back and trod it down. Rosy pushed the cross into the ground at one end.

The children stood still for a bit and then Miles said, "I could fire an arrow – sort of like a six-gun salute."

Tilly gave him a nod and he pointed his bow skyward and released the arrow. It flew in an arc over the grave and landed in the ground a few yards away.

"Good one," said Tilly.

"I know a poem Miss Cotton taught us," said Sidney.

"Really?" said Tilly, astonished.

"Sid reads books all the time," muttered Neville. "They lend 'em to 'im special like in school. Miss Cotton says 'e's clever enough to go to grammar school. Only we ain't got the money for the uniform."

Sidney shoved his hands in his torn pockets and ducked his head.

"Go on then," said Tilly.

"She told us to learn a bit of this poem about the Great War. They say it when they remember the fallen," said Sidney. "It's by Laurence Bin-somebody. I know two verses."

He put his hands straight by his side, stiff as a soldier, and recited the verses without tripping once, finishing,

"*At the going down of the sun and in the morning,*

We will remember them."

There was silence and Tilly found herself wondering why she hadn't spotted before that Sidney was actually very clever.

Then Rosy wiped her eyes and said, "That's beautiful, Sidney, thank you ever so much. Shall we say the Lord's prayer?"

Everyone nodded, and Tilly closed her eyes and put her hands together as they all murmured the familiar lines, finishing, "*...for ever and ever, Amen.*"

They opened their eyes and stood in silence for a few minutes.

Eventually Miles said, "We will always remember Tinkerbell as our first fallen soldier of the emergency zoo."

Rosy wiped a few tears away and Tilly gave her a hug, the tears welling up again in her eyes too.

Everyone bundled together their blankets and other things and set off back home. Tilly couldn't help thinking how much they had been through since she had kissed her mother goodnight the evening before.

We've built a fire and cooked our own food, slept out all night without the grown-ups, saved the pets from the enemy; but we've also buried our first pet, and we still haven't made a decision about who will look after the zoo when we're evacuated.

What on earth are we going to do? she wondered, as she waved goodbye to her friend and cycled slowly home.

Workmen were painting thick white lines around the post box, the lamp-posts and the trees in her street, but her mind was too full of worries to wonder why.

Chapter 13

A TERRIBLE STORY

Thursday morning, 31st August 1939

"Matilda Stephanie Roberts. You look like you've slept in the mud of Flanders!" cried out Mum when Tilly let herself into the house and went down to the kitchen.

Mum was standing at the scrubbed wooden table. Tilly flew into her arms, close to tears after Tinkerbell's funeral.

"Now now, you silly billy," said Mum, smoothing Tilly's hair flat against her head.

Dad came into the kitchen and said, "Where's my hug?"

Tilly turned to him and buried her face in his old woolly jumper with its tobacco and soap smell. Dad hugged her tight and lifted her off the ground.

"Did you have a topping time?" said Dad.

"Wilf," said Mum, shaking her head. "You sound like one of the children."

"It was smashing," said Tilly. "I'm starving."

Mum shook a finger at her. "You'll get your breakfast when you put on a nice clean dress and scrub those hands and face, my girl."

"Yes, Mum," said Tilly, racing from the kitchen.

The smell of bacon frying was heavenly as Tilly came back, glowing from her wash. Mum put down a huge plate of bacon, eggs and fried bread in front of her. Dad was already eating, his eyes glued to the newspaper.

"Still no word from Germany, Mother," he muttered.

"Why can't Hitler leave poor little Poland alone," said Mum, frying two more slices as Tilly wolfed her breakfast.

"Because Mr flipping Hitler wants this war," said Dad, clattering his knife and fork around on the plate. "I hope you're ready for the blackout. It starts tomorrow: Friday."

"But we're not at war yet, Dad," said Tilly.

"We soon will be."

"I've done my best, Wilf," said Mum nervously. "You know what Ted Bow's like."

Ted Bow was their local Air Raid Warden and was already patrolling the streets with a tin helmet and whistle, bossing everyone around, telling them to cover their windows.

CHAPTER 13

Dad murmured behind his paper, "Ted said something about stray pets hiding out in the old factories. He's seen the Scudder boys going that way."

He poked his head round the paper and narrowed his eyes at Tilly. "Have they said anything to you?"

Tilly felt a flutter in the pit of her stomach and her hand shook so much she nearly spilt her tea.

"No," she muttered, keeping her eyes on her plate.

"And stay away from the Scudders," said Mum, wiping her hands on her apron.

Tilly seized the chance to change the subject from hiding pets and said, "It isn't fair, Dad: Neville and the others, they're always starving. They only get a bit of bread and marge for breakfast, and sometimes no tea at all," said Tilly.

Dad gave a big sigh and put down his paper. "Bert Scudder was gassed in the trenches," said Dad. "Had a weak chest ever since – it's very hard for him to get regular work. But this war, when it comes, is going to change everything, eh Mother?"

"If you say so, Wilf."

"Oh yes," said Dad. "We men who were in the trenches, we don't want another war – we know what it means."

Mum shot Dad a frightened glance and started to pick up the empty plates.

"But there's no choice this time," Dad went on. "It'll be a fight for survival against the evil of Hitler and the Nazis. But afterwards, once it's over, you mark my words; things will have to change in this country. Working men won't put up with low wages and hungry children any more."

"And if we meet a German here—" said Tilly in a cautious voice.

Dad gave a snort. "You'd better not."

"But if it's just a boy."

"Oh, she means the Evans's little lad," said Mum, brushing a strand of hair out of her eyes. "They took in one of the Jewish children from the trains. Poor little thing. What's his name now – oh yes, Judy."

"No, Mum! It's Rudi."

"The Germans are treating their Jews very badly, so it's all right if you keep an eye on him," said Dad. "He's not the enemy."

That's a relief, thought Tilly, as she stood up to help clear the table.

Then another thought came into her mind. "What will happen to the German children's pets if there's a war?"

Dad turned the page of his paper and muttered, "Same thing as here, probably. No one wants a mad dog running amok if there's bombing."

So is it happening in all the countries? Tilly asked herself. Grown-ups murdering the children's pets. It's so horribly unfair.

Dad had gone off to work and Tilly was drying up the breakfast things when there was a knock at the door.

It was Lotte, and she was holding a small cardboard box. Tucked under one arm was a large paper carrier bag.

"Alec said to bring you this, and there is a note," said Lotte. "I cannot read it."

Tilly grabbed her and pulled her inside, hissing, "Shush! We don't want the grown-ups hearing us – they're getting very suspicious."

She pushed Lotte upstairs, calling out to Mum, "Just a friend – we're playing in my room."

Once they were in the bedroom with the door closed, Tilly took the box and opened it. Inside were two baby hamsters, fast asleep in a nest of cotton wool.

"Oh, how sweet!" she cried out, and took the note Lotte was holding out.

She saw with a thrill that it was written in code.

"Our very first message. Wait till Rosy sees this!"

On the note was written:

esaelp deef ruo seibab

"Is it English?" said Lotte, in a puzzled voice.

Tilly laughed. "Oh yes. In our code you write all the words backwards. See..." She pointed to each word and read out, "Please... feed... our... babies."

"That is so clever," said Lotte. "Hitler is mad if he thinks he can beat you English children."

She opened the bag she was carrying and said in a proud voice, "I bring this. Mr and Mrs Green, the people I work for, throw away too much food. They are very rich."

The bag was full with scraps of meat.

Tilly gave a low whistle. "Exactly what we need. Well done!"

"Maybe you can let Hanno have a tiny bit too, please?"

"Of course. We share everything."

Lotte's face broke into a smile as she looked round Tilly's room. "You have so many books. I love to read but all my books are at home. In Germany the Nazi students burnt books on huge fires."

"Burn?" Tilly was horrified. "Why would they do that?"

"They burn books by anyone they don't agree with. I saw it in Frankfurt, our city, in the *Romerplatz*. Papa pulls me away because I want to rescue the books. I was only ten. Mutti says they are barbarians."

Tilly was so shocked she couldn't speak for a minute. What would Rosy say about burning books? She looked at the little supply of books on her shelves; her birthday and Christmas presents. She pulled one out and said, "Have you read this? You can borrow it if you like."

Lotte took the book in her hands as if it was a precious jewel and read the title aloud, "*The Railway Children* by E. Nes... bit. Thank you, Tilly, you are so kind girl."

"She's my favourite author; and when you've read all my books, Rosy has loads more."

"Oh, you are a true friend, and I thank you from the top of my heart. I will write to Mutti and tell her."

Tilly nodded, and then she said, "Mum says that Rudi is Jewish. Is that why you came here?" She stopped and her cheeks flushed as the other girl lowered her eyes.

"Sorry," said Tilly, flustered, "I didn't mean to be rude."

"Oh no," said Lotte. "You are right. We are Jewish. The Nazis are very cruel to everyone, but especially the Jews. They do very bad things."

Tilly's mouth felt suddenly dry and she licked her lips. "Like what?"

Lotte hesitated and then she said in a quiet voice, "They take Papa and other Jewish men and make them cut the grass in the football stadium."

That didn't sound too bad to Tilly. "Did he use shears?" she asked.

"His teeth."

"But… I don't understand," whispered Tilly back. It sounded like some sort of a joke.

"All day and in the night, down on the knees, twenty Jewish men, they are to cut all the grass with their teeth."

Lotte's eyes were lowered and Tilly could see she had gone red with the shame of it.

Lotte continued, "When Papa come home his mouth is all bloody. He cannot speak for one week. Hitler wants to kill all the Jews."

"Can't your parents escape too?"

Lotte stared at Tilly for a moment and then she pulled a piece of paper from her pocket and opened it. "Mutti writes to me almost every day. She is worried I forget my German." She gave a little grin. Then she read aloud from the letter, "*What a lot of mistakes you are making in German. It is a good thing your English has improved so much. But don't forget everything – that would be deplorable. Think of us all here in Germany.*"

Lotte paused as if searching for something in the letter and then she said, "Oh, here it is. *Nothing is happening with us but we are prepared to leave at any time. We are trying to get permits to go to Cuba and Chile.*"

"Can't they come to England?" Tilly hadn't even heard of Cuba. Where on earth was it?

Lotte shook her head. "England has refused them." Then she put the book under her arm and said, "Now I must go. You will see Rudi later?"

"Yes, of course," said Tilly.

They went downstairs and Tilly let Lotte out.

She was just about to grab her bike and go off to the den when Mum came down the hall and handed her a piece of paper. "Shopping please, Tilly."

"But I said I'd meet Rosy." It was already eleven – the pets in the zoo would all be getting very hungry.

"Off you go," snapped her mother. "There'll be rationing soon, and I have to stock up. You should see what Mrs Benson has got in her larder. Enough to feed an army – and there's only the two of them."

Tilly gave a sigh and went outside to get her bike. She rode off to the High Street and, just as she neared the bank, she spotted the girl on the horse, Sophia Highcliffe-Barnes, wearing a pale green dress and black patent shoes. Walking ahead of her was her mother, very smartly dressed, and another woman, wearing a bright red hat.

Tilly was about to accelerate past when Sophia caught her eye and beckoned to her.

How strange, thought Tilly, but there was something about the look on the older girl's face that made her pedal over.

"Hello," she said in a cautious voice.

"Thanks ever so much for stopping," said Sophia quietly, glancing at the two women who had stopped outside the bank. "It's just the upstairs maid said her brothers had left their tortoise in a safe place... a hut in the woods..."

Sophia hesitated, and Tilly couldn't help wondering how many maids they had. But she said, "Why?"

"I thought you might be able to help me, because—"

Sophia's voice was drowned out by the rising voice of the woman in the red hat. "—this absolutely dreadful murder of our pets. There are no words for it!"

Tilly and Sophia exchanged glances.

"Aunt Edith," whispered Sophia, staring round at her mother, who had a deep frown on her face.

"Well, I suppose the upper classes might be able to save their little cats and dogs," boomed Sophia's mother, "but for goodness' sake, Edith, no one needs the flea-bitten mutts of the poor." Then Sophia's mother swept into the bank, followed by Aunt Edith, shaking her head.

"I have to go," muttered Sophia. "My mother..." and she gave a shrug.

So maybe she's not such a snob, thought Tilly. "Look, you mustn't tell the grown-ups. Promise?"

"Oh no, you can trust me, absolutely," said Sophia, her eyes wide with hope.

"All right. We're in the hut beyond the thicket at the end of the field. Our password is *doof tep.*"

Sophia gave a swift nod and ran off into the bank looking rather like a frightened rabbit herself.

It was past midday before Tilly could finally escape from Mum. She had to sneak the hamsters' box and bag of scraps out of the house. Once outside, she settled the box in her basket, hung the carrier bag over the handle bars and, pushing her bike onto the street, set off towards the canal. As she reached the towpath, she could see huge fires burning as far as the bend a quarter of a mile away. The flames lit up the water, turning it deep red.

Two workmen came past her and one said to the other, "There's 'alf a million cats and dogs in London. Are they gonna burn them all?"

They both sniffed and pushed some sacks deeper into one of the fires on the canal bank.

Tilly pedalled as fast as she could away from the horrible sight, her eyes smarting with smoke, and only stopped to catch her breath once she reached the fields. Gulping the clean air, she caught sight of a ladybird on a leaf and the old rhyme came into her mind, *Ladybird ladybird, fly away home, your house is on fire, your babies are burning.*

Shuddering, she got back on her bike and rode off to the den.

Chapter 14

PROMISE WE WON'T BE SEPARATED

Thursday afternoon, 31st August 1939

Rosy was in the clearing when Tilly arrived and called out in an excited voice, "Look! Our very first code message! And you wouldn't believe who I met on the High Street."

She waved the paper but Rosy didn't answer. Tilly could see her face was very pale as she dropped her bike in the grass. There were two bright red points on Rosy's cheeks, as if she had a fever.

"I told Megan," Rosy said in a quivery voice. "I had to – I couldn't stop crying."

"About the emergency zoo?"

"No, of course not. I said I hadn't quite told the truth about Tinkerbell – that I'd hidden her in the bushes near the canal and she'd died and we'd buried her. But oh, Tilly, we're in such trouble."

"What do you mean?"

"Megan asked me *three* times exactly where I hid Tinks and I got in such a muddle. But then she said she knew children were hiding pets in the old factories."

Tilly gasped. "That's what Dad said too, it's the rumour going round. But if they start to believe it, how long before they find the hut? It's only a few minutes away across the field."

She felt that awful chill down her spine again. First Conor finds the hideout and threatens to give us away, and now the grown-ups are closing in on us. How can we put them off the scent?

"It... it... it's much worse even than that," hiccupped Rosy, between sobs. "Megan told me that she won't let me be evacuated with the High School. She says Mummy wouldn't want us to be separated if there's a war... " Her voice broke and her face looked absolutely distraught as tears rolled down her cheeks.

Tilly was so shocked she felt her legs turn to water. It was as if a bomb had dropped between them, opening up a huge hole, separating them for ever.

"But... but..." she stammered. "Can't you make Megan change her mind? What about Donald?"

Rosy brushed the tears from her cheeks and said, "Donald didn't even give me his secret wink. I begged and pleaded until Megan got so furious with me she nearly dropped the teapot."

Rosy fixed her green eyes filled with anguish on Tilly as she said, "I want to be with you in the war, not with Megan. You're the only person in the whole wide world who really understands me, Tilly, now Mummy and Daddy are gone. We've got to stay together, haven't we?"

"Of course! Nothing will ever separate us – it's positively unthinkable! We're going to *make* the grown-ups send us away together."

Rosy's sobs calmed a bit and she said, "I feel as if I'm losing all my friends – first Tinkerbell and now you. There's no one left."

Tilly leaned over and patted her arm in desperation. "I'll come up with a plan."

But as she stared across towards the wood, a crow flapping slow and black between the trees, she felt empty of all inspiration. All she could do was try to cheer Rosy up a bit to take her mind off the impending doom.

CHAPTER 14

Tilly pushed her hair back from her face. “Well, what about Tinkerbell’s sign?” she said. “Did you make one?”

Rosy wiped her eyes with the end of her cardigan and then pointed to a flat parcel in her bike basket wrapped with brown paper and tied up with string. “I stayed up till really late doing it by torchlight under the blankets.”

“Well done. Let’s sort out the pets and then put it up.”

Rosy gave a nod and, just then, Alec came out carrying the tank. He set it down in the grass, pushed the lid aside and peered into it.

“Freddy’s dead,” he said, in a subdued voice.

Tilly could see Rosy’s mouth droop again so she thrust Lotte’s bag of scraps towards her and said, “Here, go and feed our pets.” She made sure she said “our” in a clear voice and Rosy went off inside the hut.

“She don’t look too happy,” said Alec.

“Her cat died last night and we buried her this morning. I’m so sorry about Freddy.”

Alec gave a shrug. “Don’t worry, I ain’t gonna blubber. He was a good little chap.”

“Do you want to bury him next to Tinkerbell?”

"Nah, it's all right. I'll sort him out." Alec picked up the stiff corpse, wrapped it in a piece of sacking, and pushed his way through the thicket.

Tilly went off to release Bonny, who jumped up at her, licking her hand with great joy as usual. Hanno perked up too, but when he saw no sign of Rudi, he dropped back down on his belly, his sad eyes staring up at Tilly. Then Pirate gave a loud squawk and tapped his beak on the bars of the cage. Hanno pricked up his ears and gave a loud yap back.

"What are they saying, Bonny?" said Tilly.

But Bonny ran out of the back of the hut with a loud whuff as if to say, "Come on, let's play".

Tilly followed and spotted Rosy kneeling down at Tinkerbell's grave. "Shall we put up the sign now?" she called out, walking over.

"I've done it," said Rosy.

"Oh," said Tilly. She felt a bit hurt Rosy hadn't asked her to help.

The sign was tied onto the bottom of the cross with a length of black velvet ribbon. Rosy's best ribbon, meant for church, Tilly noticed, and she wondered what Megan would say.

CHAPTER 14

On the sign, Rosy had painted a picture of Tinkerbell and written in red paint:

To my best friend and the sweetest
little cat in all the world
Tinkerbell Wilson
6th May 1935 – 30th August 1939

They stood and looked at the sign in silence for a few moments, and then Rosy stepped away from Tinkerbell's grave and bent down to pull a tiny weed from the fresh earth. With shoulders quite drooped, she wandered off back to the hut, muttering, "Better feed the little pets."

Tilly took Bonny off for a drink at the stream, partly because she didn't know what else to do for her friend, and partly because there were so many things to think about that she hardly knew where to start. As Bonny rummaged around on the edge of the stream, Tilly tried to sort everything out in her head.

They were running out of food and she was going to have to think of something soon, or all the animals would start to slowly starve. Already when she picked up Bonny for a cuddle she was sure her ribs were sticking out more than usual.

They had no one to look after the zoo yet, and now the biggest disaster of all: Rosy wasn't allowed to be evacuated.

Right – first things first, she told herself. I'll ask Alec at the next possible moment to take over the zoo next week when we leave.

But sorting out Rosy's evacuation; that seemed an insurmountable problem, and she had no idea where to start.

As she arrived back in the clearing, Bonny trotting ahead, a voice called out from the edge of the thicket, "Hello."

Tilly spun round to see Sophia pulling some brambles out of her hair, and Neville standing looking worried, hands in his pockets.

"She said the password, proper, Tills," said Neville, hands in his pockets, eyes fixed on the ground as if he expected Tilly to yell at him.

"What's *she* doing here?" shouted Miles, dropping out of a tree, followed by Sidney.

"She'll give us away," said Sidney, glowering towards Sophia. "Is your Mum with you on her horsy?" He and Miles sniggered.

Sophia was pulling a rope, and suddenly a very grumpy-looking goat burst through the bushes. It had a long beard and two pointed horns.

"Come *on*, Horace," moaned Sophia, as she tugged and tugged.

The goat had come to a complete standstill and wouldn't budge. Sophia sounded close to tears. She was wearing her riding outfit, and her cream jodhpurs were streaked with mud and brambles from the thicket.

Sophia brushed her forehead with the back of her hand and said, "Please help – I don't know who else to ask."

"How did you find us?" asked Rosy, who had come out of the hut, Toffee in her arms.

Tilly tried to meet her eye but Rosy was staring off into the distance again. The guinea pig snuffled into her jumper and then twitched his dear little nose in the air. But Rosy didn't seem to notice how endearing he looked this morning. Tilly gave an inward sigh.

"I saw Tilly on the High Street..." Sophia's voice faded away and she ran a hand through her blond hair, which was blowing in a tangle round her face.

"I gave her the password," said Tilly. She reddened a bit when she saw the boys exchanging looks.

"We can't trust her," said Miles. "She's a right snob – with her horses, and her mum called us urchins."

"I'm so sorry," murmured Sophia.

"Look," said Tilly. "I don't think Sophia has to be like her mum, does she? Are we all exactly like our parents?"

The boys mumbled under their breaths but no one challenged her.

"It's Horace," Sophia blurted out, taking advantage of the pause. "Daddy says he has to be put down. He's sending the horses down to Aunt Edith's in Sussex next week. She's got lots of stables and outhouses and things. But he says Horace is useless – you can't even eat him, he's so old." She gave a little sob and Tilly almost put out an arm to comfort her. "Horace has arthritis, poor old dear. But I don't give two hoots about their stupid war if I can't protect Horace."

"Why can't your aunty take your goat, then?" said Sidney.

Sophia shook her head. "She went back to Sussex this morning and Daddy only told me at lunch. I rode all the way here on Misty and poor Horace had to walk. It's miles and miles."

"What do you think?" Tilly said, looking round at the others.

"She said the password," muttered Neville, and Miles gave a shrug.

Tilly turned back to Sophia. "Now look here," she said. "You agree to our rules and you swear on Horace's life you will never betray us."

Sophia's eyes filled with tears. "Oh yes, I swear. I'm so grateful to you."

Tilly looked round at The Cobras and then she said, "All right then, you're in."

"Oh, thank you so much," said Sophia. "And I brought this."

She lowered a knapsack she had on her back and pulled out a huge paper bag. Opening it, she showed it to them.

"Whoopee!" cried Miles. "That's enough food for the weekend. Horace can just eat grass, can't he?"

"I suppose so," said Sophia, as she tied Horace up securely.

Horace tried to butt her with his fierce-looking horns but she patted his nose and spoke to him in a quiet voice until he calmed down.

"We'd better feed the pets and clean them out," said Tilly. She went over to Rosy and whispered, "I haven't forgotten, Rose – I promised, didn't I?"

Rosy didn't even turn to meet her eyes. But she shrugged and walked off into the hut.

Sophia joined them, exclaiming, "Goodness, did you do all this yourselves? Look at those gorgeous guinea pigs – who made their cages?"

The Scudder boys seemed to warm up after all the compliments, and proudly showed her the hinged lids they had made. Soon Sophia was picking up pets, feeding them and cleaning out the dirty bedding. Running in and out of the clearing, she pulled up huge armfuls of grass and made up fresh beds for the small pets.

Tilly tried to get Rosy interested in the baby hamsters. "Why don't you sit here and cuddle them for a bit?" She gently pushed Rosy over to a crate, settled her down with the babies on her lap and found some nice pieces of lettuce from Sophia's supply to feed them.

CHAPTER 14

The hamsters were quite delightful – one brown and one piebald, with the softest coats and tiny pink ears. They seemed to like the lettuce, snuffling around and taking tiny bites. Tilly was enchanted and had to keep Bonny back as she kept thrusting her nose towards Rosy's lap.

"No, Bonny, honestly – you'd just eat them up!" she cried out, trying to catch Rosy's eye and make her laugh. But Rosy didn't take any notice; a totally dejected look was always on her face now.

Sophia called out, "I must go. Mummy doesn't like me to ride off on my own, and I'll be in for it if I'm late home too. But thank you so much, everyone, and I'll be back in the morning to help out again. It's such fun here. I think you're all absolutely marvellous!"

With a wave, she was gone, and Miles said, "She's all right, I suppose."

"Course she is," said Sidney.

Tilly grinned at them and said, "I think it's time for us to go too. We'd better double check all the cages are properly closed for the night."

She tied up both dogs, having given Hanno some freedom to run around too. Hanno and Bonny had become firm friends and they now slept next to each other – Hanno's long brown nose resting on Bonny's back. Bonny still whined when Tilly left, but it was a comfort to know she had a friend to keep her warm at night.

Tilly popped the tortoise back in his box. Pirate tapped his beak against the cage and Hanno yapped back. Even Bonny gave a whuff, so all the pets seemed to be making friends with each other.

The Scudders and Miles had disappeared by the time she was satisfied everyone was safe for the night. Rosy was already mounting her bike, and didn't speak at all as they cycled home. They parted on the corner and Tilly arrived home more worried than ever about her friend.

As she lay in bed that night, her legs missing Bonny's warmth even more after their night together in the hut, she knew she only had a few days to sort out the emergency zoo and find a way to persuade the grown-ups to let Rosy join her in the evacuation.

Chapter 15

A CLOSE SHAVE

Friday 1st September 1939

Friday morning dawned clear and sunny like every day that week. The grown-ups called it an Indian summer; it certainly made things much easier with the zoo. How would they get all the pets out for fresh air if it rained every day?

As Tilly brushed her teeth she looked out of the open bathroom window. Sunlight dappled the ground between the trees. Everything was still and quiet, except for the clop of the milkman's horse from the street and the clink of milk bottles on doorsteps. But, from tonight, the whole country would be in blackout. Evacuation started today in London, and she'd heard on the news that the French had already sent thousands of children out of Paris.

If the whole world is blacked out, how will anyone find their way home? she wondered. A man in the queue in Woolworth's had said, "It's all very well not showing any lights, but the Thames'll be lit up like a blooming Christmas tree when there's a moon, won't it?"

So the German bombers won't get lost, she'd thought with a shudder. At least they lived a few miles from the river. Maybe the planes will run out of bombs before they get to West London. But she didn't hold out much hope.

After breakfast Dad said, "I want your help in the garden this morning; my shift starts a bit later at the works."

Tilly gave a big sigh. When on earth can I get to the zoo and feed the pets? she thought as she went outside. Dad was pushing the spade into the hard earth by the fence, his big leather boot looking like a poster in Donald's window: "Dig for Victory". It made Tilly grin as she started to pull up some weeds.

Mid-morning, Mum called them in for elevenses. Dad went in ahead, but when Tilly came through the back door calling out, "Any cake left?" there was no one in the kitchen.

What's happened? she wondered, washing her hands at the sink. Then she went down the hall to the sitting room.

Mum and Dad were listening to the wireless and, as the last tones died away, Dad switched the dial to off and they all stood there in silence.

The kettle had begun to boil on the gas and a slow whistle could be heard from the kitchen. Still no one moved.

Then Dad said, "It's the beginning, Mother."

His eyes were dark with worry and Tilly slipped her hand in his, feeling frightened, but not knowing why. Dad squeezed back, his broad comfortable hand reassuring as always, but his face didn't lighten. Something terrible had happened, but Tilly was too scared to ask what.

Mum wiped her hand across her forehead and, with a worried sigh, walked off to the kitchen, Tilly and Dad following. They sat down at the table and watched Mum lift the kettle off the gas and pour water into the big brown teapot.

"Oh Wilf," she said.

"What's beginning?" asked Tilly in a tiny voice.

"Germany invaded Poland at dawn this morning," said Dad.

Mum poured out tea and cut slices of cake.

I still don't understand, thought Tilly, but she was too scared to ask.

Dad spooned sugar into his tea and stirred it round and round until Tilly thought he would never stop. Then he said, "The Prime Minister told Germany that if they don't withdraw from Poland then we'll declare war. I'm surprised he hasn't done it already."

"Do you want him to?" asked Tilly.

"Of course. We all do – Ted Bow, Donald and even Bert Scudder, with his rotten chest." Dad's eyes narrowed and he leaned towards Tilly. "If we let Hitler get away with this, he'll bomb us anyway. Think we're too chicken to stand up to him. We have to go over there and give him a proper bloody nose. Let him know who he's dealing with, right Mother?"

"Yes, Wilf."

But Tilly could see she wasn't happy. Dad might want a war but Mum doesn't, and I don't either, not really.

Then Tilly remembered how Lotte had said in the bedroom, "Mutti says Hitler's a wild beast. Nothing will stop him."

It's because of Hitler we had to set up the emergency zoo, Tilly reminded herself. So, yes, we must beat him

– otherwise all the pets in the world might die, let alone people.

"If it's the only way to stop Hitler coming over here and bombing us, then I think we should declare war, too," said Tilly.

Dad gave her an approving nod, saying, "That's my girl. But you'll be evacuated next week with your High School friends."

Evacuated. That word again.

It was then that Tilly realized she had to be braver than she'd ever been in her life if she was going to keep her promise to Rosy.

She pushed her chair back and stood up.

"What now?" said Mum, in an irritable voice.

Tilly took a deep breath to steady herself. She couldn't meet Dad's eye so she looked down at the table cloth. "Dad, Mum, Megan has told Rosy she won't let her be evacuated and Rosy is so terribly sad. She can't bear to be parted from me because we're almost like sisters and—"

"What on earth are you talking about, you silly girl!" snapped Mum, brushing crumbs off the table cloth into her hand.

Her parents didn't even seem to be listening. Dad was finishing his piece of fruit cake. He'd leave for work in a few minutes.

"Please, Dad," Tilly went on in a trembling voice. "This is just as important as the war."

Her father frowned but he looked up, and, seizing her chance, Tilly rattled out, "I want you to tell Megan she must let Rosy be evacuated with me. I promised Rosy we'd stay together in the war; I can't break my prom—"

"How dare you speak to your father like that!" cried out Mum, banging the kettle back on the hob. "We'll hear nothing more of what you want, miss. 'I want' doesn't get!"

Tilly felt tears spring into her eyes, but she cried out, "No, Mum! I won't leave without Ro—"

Before she could say anything else, her mother slapped her hard across her bare leg.

It stung so much Tilly let out a sharp cry. She had to bite her lip to stop tears spurting out.

For a moment no one moved, as if frozen in time, staring down at the table. The tension in the kitchen was like something Tilly could almost reach out and touch. It seemed to settle on everything, layering scum over the surface of their freshly poured tea and creeping over the fruit cake.

The war's like a fiery dragon or a monster with no face, she thought with a shiver. It's going to eat us all up and there'll be nothing left.

"You'll be leaving first thing Tuesday morning," said Dad as he pushed back his chair and ran a hand back through his hair, which he always did when he was worried or annoyed. "It's up to Megan what she decides for Rosy, and I won't hear another word about it. Now go to your room."

Tilly went out of the kitchen and upstairs. She lay on her bed, tears leaking out, missing Bonny so much. If her little dog were there she'd snuggle up and comfort Tilly, lick away her tears and soothe the hot red patch on her leg where Mum had smacked it.

Why, oh why, won't the grown-ups listen to us? thought Tilly. They think they're the only ones going to war. But the children will be at war too, and I can't leave Rosy all alone. It would be utter treachery.

As tears continued to pour down her face, Tilly turned onto her side and fell asleep.

She woke up with a start to hear voices in the hall downstairs. Straining to listen, she heard Dad say, "Nothing would surprise me this week, Ted."

Has the war started? she thought, and, leaping out of bed, she went out of the door and downstairs.

"Here she is," said Mum.

Ted Bow was standing in the open doorway, wearing his ARP uniform and big black wellingtons, tin hat on his head and a whistle round his neck.

"Do we need to go to the shelter?" asked Tilly in an anxious voice.

"What for?" blustered Ted. "We haven't declared war yet."

Tilly gave a sigh of relief. She was shaking at the thought of it all starting. How will I cope when it really does? she wondered.

"Ted says some men from the council have found evidence of pets being hidden in the old factories," said Dad, glaring at her. "Now come on, Tilly, tell us the truth, mind. We can't have this nonsense going on at a time like this."

Tilly felt her blood freeze. What do they know? What can I possibly say?

"Speak up, girl," said Ted.

Nincompoop, Tilly nearly blurted out.

Think, she told herself. Then she had a brilliant idea.

"Um, well, actually me and Rosy hid Tinkerbell in the bushes beside the canal—"

"—You what!" roared Dad. "How dare you defy me?"

Tilly was shaking in her shoes and she thought she'd get another slap. " I… I… it was only… Tinks and… Rosy told Megan because she died, Tinkerbell I mean."

"Oh what a shame," said Mum. "That was the kitten her Mum gave her before *she* died."

The men shuffled their feet and huffed a bit, and Tilly kept her fingers crossed behind her back that they wouldn't ask about Bonny.

"And the factories?" asked Ted, frowning at her.

"I don't know anything about that – we're not allowed to play in there," said Tilly.

Ted shook his finger at her and said, "You make sure you tell all the children, including them Scudders – bunch of hooligans – to stay well away from the factories and come and tell us the minute you see any stray animals. The very minute – you understand me, young lady?"

"Oh yes, of course, Mr Bow," said Tilly, giving him her most serious look.

Ted walked off with Dad, who had to go to work, and as she watched them go, Tilly thought, Could war be more terrifying than having to outwit Mum, Dad *and* Ted Bow?

Chapter 16

A VISION OF HELL!

Friday afternoon, 1st September 1939

Mum disappeared off to the kitchen and Tilly made her escape before she was marched back into the garden for some more horrid digging.

Her leg was still red from the slap, and in quite a fury she grabbed her bike and went out the gate, swinging it shut with a loud bang.

The streets were very busy for early afternoon. As she rode along she had to pull up her brakes several times to avoid people crossing in front of her, and all along the pavements people were walking rapidly, heads pressed forward, as if they had an urgent appointment at the doctor. They were all carrying baskets, or pulling dogs along on leads, or holding birdcages to their chests.

Everyone has a pet with them, she thought. Where on earth are they going? Maybe they're evacuating their pets. Just then, she saw a crocodile of children from Townfield Elementary school snaking towards the railway station. Every child carried a knapsack over their shoulders and had brown labels round their necks. Cycling up to the line, Tilly could see names on the labels. The start of the evacuation, she thought.

"Where are they sending you to?" Tilly asked a tall girl.

"Wish they'd tell us," said the girl, shifting her knapsack to another shoulder. "We're off to the country, that's all I know. Hope they have ponies."

Then she was gone, and, as Tilly waited for the line to cross the road in front of her, she saw a woman with a puppy in her arms and a small boy gripping her leg and wailing.

"No, Timmy," the woman was saying. "You know what Daddy said. Fido will bark and bite people when the bombs fall and he can't come in the shelter – there's no room."

"Fido! Fido! Fido!" screamed the little boy, over and over.

People hurried on past her, clutching baskets, and Tilly followed.

A long queue was building up on the street.

"What's going on?" she asked a boy – older than her, with a rabbit in his arms.

"We're waiting for the vet to put the animals down. It's kinder. The war could start any minute now Germany's invaded Poland," said the boy. "I'll be off to the army soon anyway: they're calling up all the men and I'm already seventeen."

He looked to Tilly as though he couldn't wait. She rode to the end of the line where she could see the vet's door wide open, the waiting room full of people with their pets waiting quietly for death. It made her shudder and she pedalled away and round the next corner. There was a high fence, but in the middle was a gate which stood open. Curious, she went over and looked through the gate.

It was like a vision of hell!

Piles and piles of dogs, cats, birds and other animals were thrown together in the yard behind the vet's house, waiting for… well… she had no idea what. But it didn't matter whether they were going onto the bonfires by the canal or somewhere else. They were all absolutely, completely dead.

All those poor, unwanted animals, she thought, as tears welled up in her eyes. Dear little pets belonging to children like me and Rosy. The grown-ups didn't love them enough to look after them and feed them in the war.

"Shocking, if you ask me," came a voice in her ear and, whirling round, she saw an old man, leaning on a stick.

"What will they do with them all?" asked Tilly.

"Turn 'em into glue. Need a lot of glue in a war. Someone's going to get rich," said the old man, and he walked away, limping on one leg.

How dreadful! thought Tilly.

She turned her bike and rode off, almost blinded by tears, until she reached the fields. Pulling up her brakes, she stood for a moment, feeling the warm sunshine on her back. Swallows swooped above her head and foxgloves nodded along the hedgerow where blackberries were already ripe. A grey field mouse popped its head up to stare for a second and then, quick as a flash, disappeared into the yellow corn, which was undulating like a sea, all the way to the horizon.

Thank goodness the emergency zoo is safe, she told herself – at least for now; and she rode on to the clearing.

The others had already arrived and the little girls were playing with their pets in the grass. They were right in the middle of a clapping song she and Rosy used to do when they were little. Tilly stopped for a moment and watched them.

"*Bat, bat, come under my hat,*
And I'll give you a slice of bacon,
And when I bake I'll give you a cake
If I am not mistaken."

Then she felt a cold hand in her palm. Turning, she saw Rosy's chalk-white face – those points of red flaming away like a furnace.

"Only a few more days until you're evacuated."

"I told Dad I'd promised you we'll stay together and he must speak to Megan about you coming too," Tilly said, her chin stuck in the air defiantly.

"I bet your Mum and Dad didn't like that. Did they shout at you?" said Rosy, her green eyes flashing.

"Mum slapped my leg." She showed Rosy the red patch, which was beginning to fade.

"Oh, Tilly," Rosy breathed. "You withstood torture for me."

"It was nothing," said Tilly, but she had to admit she'd been very shocked. Her mother hardly ever smacked her.

They went into the hut and Tilly called out, "Here I am, my darling Bonny." She set her dog free and Bonny immediately started to jump up. Tilly bent over her, pulling gently on her curly ears, enjoying the feel of her dog's rough, warm tongue licking her face.

Rosy was about to say something when a high-pitched screaming came through the open door of the hut. The girls raced outside to see Horace charging across the clearing, head down, horns ready to tear into anyone near enough.

He's going to gore the girls to death, thought Tilly in horror.

"Run!" she yelled but they huddled terrified in the grass, clutching their pets and screaming.

Miles fired an arrow, which hit Horace's thick, hairy back and he let out a whoop, but it just bounced off.

Then Sidney jumped into Horace's path, yelling, "Here boy!"

He had a bit of rope in his hand and started to whistle in a shrill tone.

"He's not a sheep!" yelled Tilly. "Get out of the way, Sid."

She picked up a stone and threw it hard. It hit Horace on the tip of his nose and, for a second, the old goat halted, pawing the ground and waving his horns about. Then he lowered his head for the final charge.

Tilly was about to hurl another stone when Sophia burst through the clearing screaming out, "Horace! Stop right now!"

Horace stumbled to a halt, his horns inches from Sidney's bony legs. Then the wily old goat started a hoarse, plaintive bleating.

"You silly billy," muttered Sophia, grabbing the end of the rope which Horace had chewed through. Turning to the children she said, "I am so sorry, please forgive us – I'll make sure he never escapes again. Please, Tilly, don't send us away."

"Your stupid goat nearly killed my sister," called out Neville.

"Well, the girls seem fine now," said Tilly.

Mary and Pam had settled back in the grass, and were cooing and calming down the rabbits and the little pets. No one seemed any the worse for their latest adventure.

"Don't worry," said Tilly, feeling sorry for the older girl. "Just make sure it doesn't happen again."

Miles came over with a coiled-up piece of rope. "Found it on the dump at the back of the hut. If we double it up, it might stop him chewing through it."

Sophia, still struggling with Horace, who was trying to pull away from her, nodded breathlessly, and Miles set to work.

Tilly looked round for Rosy, but there was no sign. She was about to walk round to Tinkerbell's grave when the SOS sounded on the bugle.

Rudi burst into the clearing, his face plastered with sweat, panting hard. He pointed back towards the fields and cried out in a mixture of German and English, "Conor *kommt*... looking, looking... *ja*! *Mit dem Boxer-Hund*... *und* bad boy."

"What's he saying about Conor?" said Tilly in alarm.

"It sounds as though Conor's coming back and that creepy Bill," murmured Rosy, who had wandered over so silently Tilly hadn't even heard her.

Miles slotted an arrow in his bow. Feet wide apart he took up his position on guard.

Boxer broke through the thicket, tugging Conor behind him on the end of the chain, but there was no sign of Bill.

The dog came to a halt inches from Tilly's feet. She stood her ground, hands on hips, as furious a look as she could muster on her face, even though her knees were shaking.

Conor tugged on the lead and muttered, "Sit, Boxer, sit, boy."

When Conor raised his head, Tilly let out a gasp. His face was streaked with tears. She couldn't believe it.

"You gotta help me, Tilly," Conor said. "It's me Dad. He says he's gonna shoot Boxer in the morning with his old army pistol. I've had Boxer since he was born. He's always stood by me – growls at Dad when he goes to hit me. Dad always backs off. He's all I got in the world since me Mum died. Please, Tilly, hide him for me."

Chapter 17

THE RESCUERS

Friday afternoon, 1st September 1939

"Get out of here," snarled Miles, and to Tilly's horror, she saw that he was pointing his knife at Conor.

Then a quiet voice behind her said, "Put it down, mate – you don't want the coppers coming for you."

It was Alec, who'd arrived in the clearing, to Tilly's enormous relief.

Miles hesitated, and then he lowered the knife and stuck it back in the sheath on his belt.

Tilly glared at Conor and said, "Don't think we've forgiven you and your bullying friend. Where is he, anyway?"

"I'm truly sorry, Tilly, Honest." Conor's words came tumbling out, his voice quivering. "Bill got evacuated with the Townfield School; you won't see him no more."

"Why should we take your dog?" cried Mary.

"He's got big teeth and I'm scared of him," said Pam, on the verge of tears.

But Tilly couldn't help feeling sorry for Boxer, and even a little bit for Conor. She whispered to Rosy, "I was right – he does care about his pet."

But Rosy didn't reply. She was in her own unhappy world now, and there was nothing Tilly could do to cheer her up. Tilly felt her own spirits sinking too.

Then Alec stepped forward and Tilly realized he was actually looking at Sophia. She caught his eye and blushed.

"The way I see it," Alec said, "Conor's done some bad things, but maybe you should give him a second chance."

"I agree," said Sophia in a small voice, and Alec gave her his cheery smile.

Tilly couldn't help feeling a pang of jealousy. Oh, why doesn't he look at me like that, she thought.

"Your dog tried to eat Rudi, *ja,* mate?" snarled Sidney, looking round at Rudi.

"*Ja,*" said Rudi, pulling on Hanno's silky brown ears.

"I was a right idiot," said Conor, and he sounded truly sorry. He bent down to stroke Boxer, who'd settled in the grass at his feet and let his great jaws relax.

A steady stream of saliva dripped from the side of his mouth onto the grass.

Alec seemed to lose interest, and wandered over to Sophia, who was stroking Horace's rough hairy head. He said something Tilly couldn't hear and Sophia let out a peal of laughter.

He's so much older than us, Tilly thought. He's probably not interested in the zoo any more and it looks like Rosy isn't either. It felt as though everything was falling apart.

"What about it, Tilly?" Conor said, cutting into her thoughts.

"Say no," growled Miles. "He's just trouble."

"But we can't let Boxer be shooted," said Pam.

Conor put out his hand to Miles, saying, "Sorry I bashed you, mate. Truce?"

Miles stood there, fists clenched and then he looked round at Neville, who gave a shrug. He turned back and put out his hand. "You'd better stick to it."

"I will, promise – anything for me dog. Boxer's me whole life," said Conor.

"That's all very well," said Tilly. "But how can we be sure that Boxer won't attack the other pets in the hut?"

"He won't – I'll make sure he's always chained up when I ain't here."

Tilly gave a big sigh. What else can I do? she thought. The emergency zoo should save any pet threatened with certain death. Only, she so wished Rosy would back her up like she used to. It was lonely making decisions all by herself.

"All right, then," she said. "We'd better find a good place for him." Then she called out, "Put your pets away, everyone. Timc to go home. The grown-ups are very jumpy about the first blackout tonight. We don't want them asking any awkward questions if we're out late."

"I could walk part of the way with you," she heard Alec say to Sophia.

"That would be very nice," said Sophia, blushing even more. "But I have my horse here." She disappeared off through the thicket.

Alec looked rather downcast and Tilly took her chance, saying to him in a low voice, "I wanted to ask you if you could look after the zoo when we're evacuated next week."

Alec stared after Sophia and muttered, "I suppose so."

"You'll be able to, er, chat to Sophia a bit more too, won't you?"

Alec brightened up at this and said, "All right, good idea, Tilly. Don't you worry about your pets – you can rely on me."

Then he pushed his cap to the back of his head, shoved his hands in his pockets and walked off, whistling in his cheery way.

That's one problem solved, thought Tilly, with relief. Now I just have to sort out Rosy.

The rest of the children had settled their pets down and disappeared.

Tilly found a huge iron ring bolted to the side of the hut, behind the low wall where the boys had slept the other night. "I think that'll hold him," she said to Conor, tugging hard on the ring.

"Right oh," said Conor. He chained Boxer to the ring, checked it was secure, put a tin with water down in front of him and then walked off too.

Tilly spent her final few moments alone with Bonny. She found it harder and harder to leave her little dog each day, and even though Bonny seemed happy to cuddle up with Hanno, she still whined each time Tilly walked away. She could hear the high-pitched, heart-breaking sound all the way through the thicket and as far as the field.

She gave Bonny a final kiss on her nose, promised she would be back as soon as she could and went out, closing the door behind her.

Rosy was waiting for her and they rode off in silence. As they crossed the canal Tilly called out, "Alec's agreed to look after the zoo when we're evacuated – isn't that a relief?"

But Rosy didn't respond. She cycled on into the street and Tilly trailed behind wondering what Mum would say if she sneaked back to the hut and stayed another hour. She almost collided with Rosy's bike, which had come to a halt ahead of her.

Rosy had jumped down and was standing with her head cocked on one side. "Did you hear that?" she whispered.

"What?"

Rosy dropped her bike on the kerb and ran to the door of a dilapidated house. Some of the windows were broken and paint was peeling off the front door.

Does anyone live here? Tilly wondered. "I can't hear anything," she said.

"Shhh," said Rosy, with her finger to her mouth.

They stood there in silence for a moment and then a faint sound came from inside the house. Tilly couldn't make out what it was.

But Rosy cried out, "There!"

Before Tilly could stop her friend, Rosy pushed hard on the front door, which opened with an eerie creak, and disappeared into the house.

"No, Rosy!" Tilly called out. "Come back!" But there was no answer.

I'd better follow, she thought, stepping through the open door, her nerves jangling.

Inside it was so dark and gloomy Tilly couldn't see to the end of the hall. There were no carpets and her feet echoed on the bare boards. She peered into the first room. It was completely empty and the windows were covered with peeling brown paper. For a second, Miles's "ghost with no face" flashed into her mind and, with a shiver, she turned back and walked to the bottom of the stairs.

"Rosy?" she called out in a loud whisper, terrified someone would discover them trespassing. "We shouldn't be in here."

But there was just silence.

What should I do? she thought, not really wanting to search the ghostly old house.

Then she heard footsteps above and Rosy appeared at the top of the stairs.

She'd taken off her cardigan and wrapped it round something cradled in her arms. Slowly, she came down, one step at a time. When she reached the bottom, Tilly could see Rosy's green eyes shining for the first time since Tinkerbell had died.

"What is it?" whispered Tilly.

Very gently, Rosy unpeeled a corner of the cardigan. A furry black face appeared, with tiny pointed ears and blinking eyes.

"Oh Rosy," breathed Tilly. "What a sweet little kitten."

"Isn't she?" beamed Rosy. Then the words came tumbling out. "Donald said at breakfast, you see… people are driving off to the country, to escape the bombs, with all their furniture and things, piled and piled in their cars, and Donald said they just abandon their pets—"

"—on the streets?"

"Oh yes, he's seen poor little dogs howling and trying to run after the cars—"

"How dreadful! The cruel beasts!"

"I know – and Donald said he's heard they even dump pets in empty old houses. So I knew, I just knew, when I heard the mewing outside – oh, poor little Dorothy." Rosy bent down and kissed the kitten's tiny ear.

"Jolly good name," said Tilly with a grin. "*Wizard of Oz*. At least you didn't call her Cowardly Lion."

"Or Tin Man," said Rosy, grinning back.

"Wicked Witch of the East."

"You can't call a cat a witch," said Rosy, in her most prim Megan voice, and they both burst into laughter.

"The poor mother and two babies are dead upstairs."

"Shall I go and get them?" asked Tilly, even though she really didn't want to go any further into the old house.

"No," said Rosy, walking towards the door. "Let's go, we have to look after the living now."

They went out and retrieved their bikes, Rosy laying Dorothy very carefully in her basket and talking to her all the time. "...and I'll give you a big dish of milk when we get home, and then you can sleep in my bed with me, so you won't ever be alone again."

"What about Megan?" asked Tilly as they rode off.

"I'll hide her – she'll never know," declared Rosy. "I'll bring her to the zoo tomorrow, but I'm not leaving her there. We'll never be parted."

"Brilliant," sighed Tilly. "I do so wish I could smuggle Bonny into the house, but she's much too big. I miss her every second I'm not with her."

Rosy pulled up her brakes and Tilly wobbled to a stop next to her. "You've been such a brick, Tills," she said in a serious voice. "I'm sorry I've been so awful since Tinkerbell died. Best friends still?"

Tilly stared into Rosy's anxious eyes for a few seconds and then she said, "Don't be such a nincompoop!"

They both laughed until tears streamed down their cheeks.

Chapter 18

VERY BAD NEWS

Saturday morning, 2nd September 1939

"Everyone says there's going to be a storm tonight," called out Miles, as Tilly and Rosy arrived in the clearing after breakfast. "I've been checking the hut for leaks."

Miles was leaning against the hut wall with his rat, Domino, sitting up on his hand, long whiskers quivering in the morning sunlight.

Rosy dropped her bike and called out, "We have a new addition to the zoo. Cobras – meet Dorothy."

Everyone crowded round as Rosy, her cheeks pink and shiny, showed off her little kitten.

"Ooh Mary, look at 'er tiny paws – ain't they sweet?" said Pam, stroking Dorothy as she lay like a miniature princess in Rosy's arms. Giving a tiny yawn, the kitten let out a tinkly mewing sound and the girls shrieked in delight.

"She can come and play with Antony and the baby hamsters," offered Mary, reaching out to take the kitten, but Rosy drew back.

"Maybe later," she said, smoothing down the black fur on Dorothy's back. Dorothy screwed up her eyes and wrinkled her tiny nose. "She's still in shock, I think, from being abandoned without hope." She dropped a kiss onto one ear and the kitten mewed again.

"She definitely knows you're her mum," said Tilly.

Rosy beamed round at everyone.

Rosy's back to her old self now she's got a new kitten to take care of, Tilly told herself with a happy sigh, as she announced, "I'm going to try my gas mask on in front of Bonny so she gets used to it and isn't scared."

Mary clapped her hands in delight. "Me too – come on, Pam."

Sidney and Neville exchanged raised eyebrows, but very soon everyone had pulled out their gas masks from the small square boxes they carried everywhere, and were pulling them on.

We all look like monsters from outer space, thought Tilly, as she gazed around the clearing, but it was impossible to laugh under the mask. A horrid taste of rubber was in her mouth and she felt as though she could hardly breathe.

Miles swam into view and said something, but she couldn't understand a word. He took out Domino and loomed over him, the long nose cone almost touching the rat, but Domino just stared back.

Tilly tiptoed into the hut and called out Bonny's name. The little dog started a high-pitched frantic yapping as soon as she saw the mask.

"It's all right, Bonny Bonbons," she called out. Her voice sounded as though it was under water. It took a few minutes before Bonny recognized her, and then she tried to lick Tilly's face through the mask.

"Stop it," she cried out and, ripping the mask off her head, she laughed as a delighted Bonny licked her thoroughly all over. Then she straightened and said, "Come on, let's go down to the stream for a paddle."

They went outside and Tilly called to Rosy to join them. It was much more fun in the wood without their gas masks on. Rosy sat on the bank, cradling Dorothy and talking softly to her, while Tilly splashed about in the water with Bonny. They could hear the boys egging each other on as they climbed higher and higher in the trees around the clearing.

As the morning passed, the sky grew darker, and Tilly could see clouds rolling in between the trees.

"It must be nearly lunchtime," she said, stepping out of the water. "Let's see if Alec's arrived yet."

But when they arrived back in the clearing there was no sign of Alec.

Sophia had arrived and she was feeding carrots to Horace. "Are you being evacuated?" she called out to Tilly.

"Yes," said Tilly – only she still felt so unsure. "How about you?"

"Oh, no one ever tells me anything. Aunt Edith is coming up from Sussex on Sunday, so I'm going to ask her quietly if she will take Horace when the horses go down. Daddy will be awfully angry with me but I don't care."

Sophia tossed her blond hair back, which was beautifully groomed this morning – like her horse, Tilly thought with an inward grin – and stuck her lower lip out, but Tilly could see the worry in her eyes. She's not used to standing up to her parents either, she thought with some sympathy.

"Your Aunt Edith sounded as though she didn't agree with all the animals being killed," she said.

"No, I'm sure she doesn't. I think she's in some sort of animal rescue organization – the Dumb Animal something or other – but I don't know much about it."

"Well, Alec said he'd take over the zoo, so I think our pets will be safe."

Sophia's eyes brightened and she looked at Tilly with admiration. "That's marvellous. So Horace will have a safe home whatever happens. You're a jolly good leader, Tilly. You always think of something. Must dash." Sophia headed off back to the field where she had left her horse, Misty, grazing.

Tilly watched her go with a sigh. If I'm such a good leader, she wondered, why haven't I come up with a plan to persuade Megan to let Rosy be evacuated? It seemed that their problems were just endless, and the war hadn't even started yet.

Rosy came to the door of the hut and held out her hand. "Is it raining?"

"Maybe the storm's coming."

"We should go home. Dorothy might catch a cold if she gets wet." Rosy's face looked worried again as she started to wrap the tiny kitten in a piece of clean blue flannel.

"I think you're right," said Tilly. "Everyone listen." The children looked round. "Put the pets away so they don't get wet and cold, and then get off home before the storm."

They all hurried round to settle the pets down.

Tilly tied Bonny up and gave her a last cuddle. "I'll come back as soon as I can, my darling." Bonny started to whine and whuff in a hurt tone almost immediately.

The rain held off as they cycled away and parted on the other side of the canal. As Tilly let herself into the house, she wondered with a sigh what on earth she would do all afternoon and evening without Bonny to play with. At least I won't have to dig the garden, she told herself.

Instead, Mum made her help to sew big cushions for the air raid shelter.

"We have to have something to sit on or we'll all get very damp," grumbled Mum. "It's going to be perishing down there at night. Everyone's worrying about the rationing. I bought a quarter of Bourneville cocoa and a bag of sugar this morning. The woman in front asked for ten bags and they gave it to her. Can't think what she wants with all that."

Tilly tried to nod in the right places as Mum threaded her needle again. Who cares about sugar when we have pets to save, she wanted to say.

"Once we're down in those shelters," Mum went on, "Heaven knows how I'll keep your feet dry. You know what your father's cough is like when it's damp."

If a bomb falls on us, Tilly suddenly thought, we might be buried alive underground in that horrible shelter, and there won't be any air to breathe. Just like when we put on our gas masks. She knew Neville was worried Pam might refuse to wear one. She'd only kept it on for a few seconds this morning.

Breathing, Tilly decided, was going to be one of the problems once this war started. She stabbed her needle into the thick material again. She'd much rather be with Bonny – even in the middle of a storm.

Just when Tilly was certain she was on the point of dying of boredom, a loud knock came on the front door.

"I'll go," she cried out and, jumping up, she rushed down the hallway.

CHAPTER 18

Lotte stood on the step. "I have very bad news," she whispered, her eyes burning in her pale face.

Tilly pulled her inside and called out, "It's just a friend from school."

They rushed upstairs and, once safely in the bedroom with the door closed, Tilly said, "What is it?"

"Rudi lives next door to Mrs Benson and her son, Alec, yes?" said Lotte.

Tilly nodded and a funny feeling rolled around the pit of her stomach.

"Rudi tells me now," Lotte went on, "that Alec is in the hospital with a broken leg. It happened this morning at the zoo. He fell off a ladder."

"Oh no!" cried out Tilly. "Alec's supposed to look after the pets when we're evacuated." She felt as though the sky had fallen on her.

"What will you do?" asked Lotte.

"I… I'm not sure," stammered Tilly. "I'll have to think of something."

"Please try, Tilly. I am so scared again for Rudi, and so worried…" her voice dropped, "for Mutti."

"Is your Mum all right?" asked Tilly.

"I do not get letter from Mutti this week."

"Oh dear."

Lotte pulled a tissue-thin sheet of blue airmail paper out of her pocket and said, "She write this on Friday August 25th and no more since. I shall read some to you?"

"Of course," said Tilly.

Lotte read aloud slowly, translating into English as she went along.

"*I have learnt your last letter off by heart. Please write as often as possible. We have not had a letter for days and am longing for news of you both. Tell Rudi to enjoy the summer holidays. Here in Frankfurt the children are already in school and they are not so pleased about it. Try not to worry. Keep cheerful. A whole lot of kisses from Papa and me.* "

"If Britain declares war," Lotte said, more tears falling down her face, "maybe Mutti cannot write any more and I am left alone with Rudi. Please, Tilly. We must save Hanno for my poor little brother."

Yes, we must, thought Tilly, feeling so sad for Lotte and her family, separated at such a terrible time. They were all missing each other so much and trying hard to be brave about it.

And what about my darling Bonny – lying in that old hut, waiting for me? All the animals are depending on us for food and water and friendship.

Then she had an idea. "Lotte, you won't be evacuated, will you? Why don't you look after the zoo?"

"Oh no, I could not do that. I am so sorry but I do not have much time out of the house. I have to work more and more now." Lotte stared at Tilly with her large brown eyes and then she said, "Your friend, Rosy, can she do it? Will she go away too?"

Tilly shook her head. "It doesn't look like it. I'll ask her, of course, but honestly, I don't think she could manage all those animals, cleaning the cages and bringing food every day. It's such a big responsibility."

Anyway, thought Tilly, how can I ask Rosy to look after the zoo? It would mean I've given up trying to get her evacuated with me.

"I must go," said Lotte. "Please think of something, Tilly. You always do."

They went downstairs and Tilly let Lotte out of the front door.

Her mother called her to lay the table for tea. Dad came home muttering about the Prime Minister not declaring war yet.

Mum banged the pots about and said the waiting was killing her. Why didn't they make their minds up? "Mrs Benson said the girl in the draper's said Hitler must have given up because they haven't sold any blackout curtains for a couple of days." She shot a frightened glance at Dad. "She says they're painting the post boxes some funny colour and when it changes to something or other, then you know there's gas."

"What if you're nowhere near a post box?" said Tilly.

"Oh, for Heaven's sake, Mother!" blasted Dad, and they both stopped in their tracks. Dad didn't shout very often, except when he was really angry.

"I've told you not to take any notice of that stupid woman. Hitler's not giving an inch, do you understand me? The Prime Minister will declare war today or tomorrow. He can't hold out any longer."

Tilly nodded, staring at him wide eyed. Maybe the war had already started and he was keeping it secret from them so that Mum wouldn't get even more upset.

CHAPTER 18

Tilly could hardly eat anything at tea – she was so worried about gas falling and getting food to the zoo and being evacuated. She was sure she was going to hate anywhere they sent her, because she wouldn't have Rosy or Bonny with her.

I feel just like Rosy – I'm losing all my friends too, she told herself, almost choking on her bread and butter. She was so upset she forgot to hide away bits of ham for Bonny.

After tea they sat in the sitting room. Tilly tried to read her book, but it was hard to concentrate. The window was open onto the street and the rain was falling steadily now.

It was beginning to get dark and they heard Ted Bow call out, "Nearly blackout. Turn them car lights out."

The driver called back, "Don't worry, mate, the Germans won't be here for ten minutes and I'll be home by then."

"Cheeky devil," muttered Dad, and he pulled the window shut and then closed the blackout curtains.

Tilly felt stifled in the sitting room, cut off from the world beyond. She longed to be outside in the cool night air. Her head began to ache and the words in her book danced before her eyes. One thing she was certain of: if this was war, it was going to be very, very boring.

Then, suddenly, there came what sounded like a massive explosion outside and all the windows rattled.

Tilly leapt to her feet as Mum shrieked out, "The bombing's started." She grabbed Tilly's hand and said, "Down to the shelter, now!"

"Wait," said Dad and he pulled aside the thick curtains. "Look, it's just the storm. They said the weather would break tonight."

"Oi, shut that curtain!" came a voice in the street.

It was Ted Bow again. Tilly spotted him for a second when the lightning flashed, tin hat pulled low over his head.

Like the man with no face, she thought.

They stood there in the living room, staring at each other – Mum's face creased with fear, Dad brushing his hand back through his hair, over and over again, tense with anger and worry.

This is what it will be like when the war starts, thought Tilly; the grown-ups shouting orders and terrified, the pets all alone and everyone crammed underground in the shelters without any air.

She practised holding her breath for the rest of the evening and thinking about what she was going to say to Rosy in the morning.

Chapter 19

WAR!

Sunday 3rd September 1939

Sunday morning was bright and clear after the dreadful storm which had raged most of the night. Tilly pulled aside the blackout curtains at her bedroom window and looked out into the street. The road was littered with leaves and branches blown off the trees, but the sun was shining, winking in the puddles on the pavements.

When she came down to breakfast Dad said, "The Prime Minister is speaking at eleven o'clock. You stay in, Tilly, and help your mother this morning. I want us all together to hear this."

I won't get to the zoo for ages, Tilly thought, but she didn't want to miss the news either.

Then a knock came on the back door. It was Mrs Benson. "Can't stop," she called out in the same cheery voice as Alec. "I've got a message for Tilly from Alec. He says sorry. Goodness knows what he means."

Tilly shrugged and Mum called out, "How's that leg of his doing?"

"Up to his hip in plaster. Doctor says he won't be walking for weeks – and war about to start. Must dash, Ted Bow give me a right telling off about my blackout last night."

With that, she disappeared, and Mum started to fill the sink for the washing up. Dad went out in the garden and soon they could hear him banging a few last nails into the shelter.

Tilly helped her mother for the next couple of hours until Dad came back in and said, "It's nearly time."

Mum glanced at the clock and so did Tilly. Two minutes to eleven. Without another word, they all went into the sitting room and Dad switched on the radio.

It turned out that the broadcast wouldn't be until quarter past eleven, so they sat there waiting quietly. All the families they knew up and down the street were probably gathered around their radios just like them, waiting for war to start.

Then the solemn tones of Mr Chamberlain, the Prime Minister, came on the radio and, at first, Tilly found it hard to follow until she heard the worst words of her life.

"*...I have to tell you that no such undertaking has been received and that consequently this country is at war with Germany.*"

Tilly felt herself go numb.

Dad murmured, "This is it, Mother."

Mr Chamberlain continued, "*You can imagine what a bitter blow it is to me that all my long struggle to win peace has failed...*"

"What about us?" called out Dad. "It's a ruddy bitter blow to us, mate."

"Wilf!" said Mum. "Language."

But Tilly didn't care.

We're at war, she told herself, over and over. This is the hugest moment of my life so far.

But what about my darling Bonny?

They listened to the end as the Prime Minister finished by saying, "*Now may God bless you all. May He defend the right. It is the evil things we will be fighting against – brute force, bad faith, injustice, oppression and persecution – and against them I am certain that the right will prevail.*"

Tilly didn't understand all the words, but she knew that Lotte and Rudi had already seen brute force and injustice in their home in Frankfurt and, although they had come to England to be safe, what would happen to Jewish children like them, if the Nazis invaded London? What would happen to all the children and the people and—

Before she could finish these difficult thoughts, the most blood-curdling wail went up outside and Mum cried out, "The air raid sirens!"

Without thinking, Tilly ran to the front door, wrenched it open and raced down the path, looking up at the sky. Mum and Dad were close behind. The street filled up with the neighbours – everyone craning their necks upwards.

Little Bobby from opposite came out, parading with a toy rifle, pistol, tin hat and gas mask, shouting, "Here come the Germans! Here come the Germans!"

"Look! A barrage balloon!" cried Mrs Benson.

Tilly watched as the huge silver cigar shape slowly rose in the sky – the size of a cricket pitch, Dad had said.

"That'll stop the bombers," someone called out.

"No they won't, they just put them off," came the cry back.

"Why doesn't someone just throttle Hitler?" groaned someone else.

"I'd rather be killed outright," said Mrs Benson, "than be mutilated and buried alive."

Ted Bow came puffing down the street, blowing his whistle, tin hat bumping on his head, yelling, "In the shelters, the lot of you. Come on! Look lively!"

A policeman raced past at top speed on his bicycle, crying out, "Take cover! Take cover!"

Suddenly, people were shouting to each other and grabbing children.

Mum turned and started to run back down the path, but Dad took her arm and Tilly's hand saying, "No running, Mother. We don't want the neighbours to think we panicked." Dad called out to Mrs Benson to come with them.

Tilly's knees were knocking from fear, and all she wanted was to throw herself down in the shelter and stay there for ever. How would Bonny feel when she heard the sirens? The noise went on and on, filling every part of her head. How soon before the first bomb fell on them?

As soon as they had all settled on the wooden benches in the shelter, Dad pulled the door shut and fastened it with a heavy wooden latch. The sirens wailed on and on as Tilly and her Mum clutched each other and Mrs Benson sat with her hands over her ears. There were puddles of water on the floor from last night's rain and Tilly felt chilled right through. Dad had lit an oil lamp and she tried to focus on the flame as it flickered behind the glass.

Then, just as suddenly, the siren stopped and a new tone, much calmer, sounded the All Clear.

Dad muttered, "Blooming false alarm, I'll bet. Probably just that Ted Bow showing off."

"Thank goodness," sighed Mum, wiping her hand across her forehead.

Tilly stood up, impatient to get outside, as Dad levered back the wooden latch. Catching Mrs Benson's eye, she said, "What about Alec?"

"Don't worry, pet," said Mrs Benson, in her cheerful voice. "He's safe in the hospital. They wouldn't dare bomb there, would they?"

Tilly couldn't see how they would know it was a hospital from high up in the sky above London, but she didn't say anything.

Everyone pulled themselves out and Mum went to make some tea. Tilly was desperate to go and see Bonny and finally, after lunch, which she could hardly swallow, she managed to persuade Mum to let her go out for some fresh air.

"Just a couple of hours, mind," said Mum, clattering pots around in the sink as if she was bashing Hitler's head. "And stay close to the house – the sirens could go off any time. We're at war now."

As if I need reminding, thought Tilly, as she grabbed her bike and set off down the road. She had to weave her bike through the crowds that were heading towards the vet's on the High Street. Someone called out that the queue was half a mile long.

All the pets of London are being rounded up and killed, she told herself.

But now she had to face Rosy and ask her to look after the zoo, and she was completely dreading it.

Chapter 20

TILLY TAKES CHARGE

Sunday afternoon, 3rd September 1939

When Tilly arrived at the hideout, she could hear Sidney yelling to Miles, "Betcha they land next week!"

"Don't be daft!" yelled back Miles. "My Dad says the Navy won't let the Germans put a toe in the Channel."

There was no sign of Mary or Pam and she couldn't see Horace either, which was strange. Rudi was murmuring to Hanno in German.

Tilly went into the hut to find Rosy cuddling Dorothy, her face streaked with dried tears.

"I had the most dreadful row with Megan this morning," she said, as Tilly set Bonny free and pulled her onto her lap for a cuddle. "We literally screamed at each other over breakfast. Me and Megan are totally at war because she won't let me be evacuated with you. I can't believe how horrible she is!"

"I'm afraid there's more bad news," said Tilly and she told Rosy about Alec's broken leg.

"So there's no one left to save the emergency zoo," said Rosy, and she bent over Dorothy, smoothing down the fur around her eyes and mouth.

"I was wondering..." said Tilly, "if... well... you would like to do it."

But she felt so mean as soon as she said it. Rosy turned towards her, a look of complete horror on her face.

"Me?! But I couldn't *possibly* do that all by myself." Her voice was trembling and her green eyes were filling with tears. "What if Boxer escaped and bit off my leg or Mary's rabbit scratched my face and... and... what about food? Where would I get seed for the parrot? And I haven't a clue about what to do when the tortoise hibernates..."

"No, of course not. It's all right, Rosy, I understand – really I do."

Tilly wished she'd never said anything. They sat together in a miserable silence for what seemed ages.

Then Rosy burst out, "I can't stand the thought of staying with Megan all through the war. Oh Tilly, let's run away and take Dorothy and Bonny with us. At least we can save *them*. And we could let the small pets go free. They would graze in the clearing, wouldn't they? and make nests—"

"—to hide from the foxes. I must admit, I'd been thinking the same thing. Setting them free and giving them a chance to survive."

They sat in silence again as they both digested this thought, and then Tilly said, "If we did decide to run away, where would we go?"

"What about…" began Rosy, "…asking Sophia if she knows somewhere near her aunt's house in the countryside where, perhaps, we could go with our pets and have a little room in a barn and sleep on straw and help out the farmer for our food, feeding the chickens—"

"—and collecting the eggs. Oh, it's a smashing idea, Rosy. Let's do it. Sophia must be around here somewhere, because Horace isn't in his usual place. But as soon as she arrives we'll—"

"Sophia's gone," said Miles, coming into the hut. He was holding out a piece of paper. "She left a note."

Miles handed her the note and she read it aloud.

Dear Cobras,

I hope you are all well. The most marvellous news: I've managed to persuade Aunt Edith to take Horace to her house in the countryside. Then Daddy came in and said me and Mummy are going to be evacuated tomorrow morning to Aunt Edith's anyway. So I have collected Horace to get him ready for his awful journey. I'm certain he'll get very carsick in the van.

I wanted to thank all of you, and especially Tilly, for all your kindness to me and Horace. I do hope you find safe homes for all your pets.

Good luck!

Yours sincerely (it's so much nicer than faithfully, don't you think?),

Sophia Highcliffe-Barnes.

"What a traitor," said Miles. "We should lock her up in the Tower and cut off her head."

But he didn't seem too bothered, as he ran outside, calling to Sidney and Rudi to play fighter planes.

Tilly heard Rudi say, "*Ja, komm hier, Hanno.*"

Sidney called back in what sounded like perfect German, "*Ja, gut, braver hund.*"

"Well, that's one less animal to worry about," said Tilly with a sigh. "Isn't she lucky having somewhere so lovely to go?"

Rosy nodded and the girls went outside with their pets.

Miles came over, bending down to catch his breath, and Tilly said, "What are you going to do with Domino when you're evacuated?"

"Made him a special box with holes in it. Fits at the bottom of my case. I'm taking him with me. I've told my partner, Steven dumbo Fuller, if he gives me away I'll cut his ears off." Miles brandished his knife.

"Are you taking your knife with you?"

"Course. Scout Leader says the Boy Scouts will be needed if the Germans invade. I'm hoping to get a billet with a farmer and get him to teach me how to shoot."

"Might do the same, mate," said Neville. "We're all going in the morning – no idea where."

As the afternoon wore on and it got later and later, no one made a move to go home. Tilly knew that she'd be in trouble for missing tea, let alone if the bombing started. But now they were properly at war and none of their problems were solved.

CHAPTER 20

The sun was going down, turning the sky red, and it seemed to Tilly that everything was changing around her so quickly. The streets, the sky, even her home had all become somewhere to be afraid of, instead of safe and familiar.

But the biggest fear was how she was going to save the pets *and* get Rosy evacuated with her.

There must be something we can do, she thought in desperation. There must.

Everyone sat together in the grass outside the hut as the long shadows of the evening darkened the wood behind them and the cool air began to chill their skin. The pets ran about from child to child, and only Rosy was missing as she sat behind the hut at Tinkerbell's grave.

Perhaps for the last time, thought Tilly, if we're running away tonight. If we can't ask Sophia for help, we'll have to throw ourselves on the mercy of some farmer's wife.

Just as the last ray of sun left the circle, there was a noise behind them. Conor appeared, bashing away at the undergrowth with a huge stick.

"I've come to get Boxer. We're going away with me big brothers, potato picking in Scotland. We got a lift in a lorry. We're leaving tonight," Conor said, as he went into the hut. He came out a few minutes later with Boxer straining forward on his chain.

"Well, good luck then," said Tilly, not really sorry to see the big, scary dog leave. That was one less problem to deal with.

"Thanks a million, Tilly," muttered Conor, and then he leaned forward and gave her a surprising soft kiss on the cheek.

Miles and Sidney let out piercing wolf whistles and Tilly went bright red as Conor pushed off through the thicket.

"It's time to go home, Tilly," Rosy said. "What else can we do?"

But as she stared after Conor and thought about that kiss, Tilly found a whole new idea blossoming in her mind. Conor liked her, it seemed, and she liked Alec, but *he* liked Sophia. And what had Sophia said? That Aunt Edith liked animals and was even a member of a League that protected animals. So maybe…

"I might have a plan," she said, looking round the group of children.

"I knew it! You're the best leader in the world!" cried out Rosy, and her face lit up. "Come on, tell us."

"Hmm, well, I don't know if it'll work," Tilly went on. "But I think we should go to Sophia's house tonight and blag our way in somehow – I'll need you, Sid..."

Sid gave a serious nod.

"We find Sophia's Aunt Edith. Remember, Sophia said she was staying with them this weekend."

"Why this Aunt Edith?" asked Miles.

"Oh, I get it. Brilliant," said Rosy.

"Well I don't," muttered Neville.

"Listen!" Tilly almost shouted. "We find Aunt Edith and tell her we want her to take *our* pets to the country too. She's clearly got enough room, and I think she might be a proper pet lover, like us, because she wanted to save Horace's life. It's so unfair that Sophia has somewhere to keep Horace safe and our London pets are in such terrible danger. Who's with me?"

Everyone cheered and cried out *Doof tep* until Rosy spoke over them in her clear voice, "That's all very well, but how will we get there? Donald delivers to their house each week, and it's miles away. I've been in the holidays. We can't bike there – it would take all night."

"Anyways, I can't come," muttered Neville. "Gotta 'elp Mum with the baby – Pam's too small to be much use. But Sid'll get you there. Ask Len, right?"

Sidney nodded. "Anyone got any dosh?"

They all rummaged in their pockets. Miles pulled out a shilling and a sixpence and handed it to Sidney.

"It ain't enough," said Neville. "Len'll take you in the fruit lorry, but you gotta pay 'im 'alf a dollar at least. Anyone got a shilling?"

They all shook their heads and then Rudi held out a shiny coin. It was a shilling. Now they had two shillings and sixpence for Len.

Or half a dollar, thought Tilly.

Sidney whooped and grabbed it. "*Ja*, Rudi. *Danke,* me old son."

Rudi gave a polite bow.

Sidney gave a snicker and bowed back, and then Rudi's face broke into a lovely smile Tilly hadn't seen before. They bowed to each other over and over until Sidney collapsed, laughing and rolling on the floor.

It was agreed that Tilly, Rosy, Sidney, Miles and Rudi would all go to Sophia's. They quickly put their pets away for the night and set off on their bikes, Rudi sitting on Sidney's saddle as Sid stood on his pedals, puffing away, pulling them both out of the clearing.

Speeding in the dark across the fields behind Neville, with only a thin moon to give them a tiny bit of light, Tilly kept telling herself, I've got to *make* Aunt Edith take the pets somehow. This is our last chance to save the emergency zoo.

They reached the factories and, as they pedalled towards the canal, Tilly saw how dark the streets and houses were – without even a pinprick of light. Everywhere looked so strange and unfamiliar in the blackout, it would be easy to get lost.

As they flew over the bridge and onto the street, Miles cried out, "Don't hit a lamp-post. Look out for the white lines."

Sure enough, Tilly could see thick lines painted round the trees and lamp-posts, and even the post box. How clever, she thought – that was what the workmen were doing last week. There were even white lines on the kerbs to guide the cars.

She rode on behind Miles until they all skidded to a halt outside the Scudders's tenement building. Neville went inside and Sidney raced across the yard to find Len. He was gone for what seemed like ages, and Tilly began to lose hope.

She was just deciding that she would have to bike all the way alone in the dark when Sidney reappeared, running to keep up with a stocky man in short sleeves and braces striding over the yard, cigarette burning at the corner of his mouth.

"Come on, you lot," said Sidney.

"Well done, Sid," Tilly said, as they followed Len to a lorry parked at the side of the road.

The back was open to the sky, and so high off the ground Len had to give them a leg up. There was a rather earthy pile of sacks covering the rough wood floor.

"This'll do, eh Tills?"

"Smashing, Sid."

The sound of the engine started up and the lorry moved slowly away.

"Can't go fast in the blackout, Len says, but he were right pleased when I give 'im the money," said Sidney.

"How long will it take to get there?" asked Miles. "I'm going to cop it from Mum and Dad, it's getting so late."

"It takes Donald twenty minutes in daylight, so probably more than half an hour at this rate," said Rosy.

She had Dorothy with her and Tilly could hear the kitten mewing.

I so wish Bonny was here, she couldn't help thinking. This could be our last night together for ages and ages. The thought made her so sad she was almost ready to cry.

Then Sidney pressed an apple into her hand. "Len says we can 'elp ourselves – got some left over from market this morning."

Tilly bit into the juicy apple and realized that she'd hardly eaten anything all day. They had three apples each, and then she felt much better.

They rolled on out of town and along roads with trees meeting overhead. It was so dark they couldn't see their hands in front of their faces. Sidney and Miles made ghostly noises, and even Rudi joined in. Rosy put Tilly's hand on Dorothy's warm body, and Tilly felt a bit comforted as her stomach filled with nervous flutters.

"How much longer?" called out Miles as they hit a bump in the road.

Before Rosy could answer, the lorry came to a halt with a squeal of brakes.

They were in a dark lane and the outline of huge gates could be seen overhung with trees.

"That's the drive. We have to walk from here," said Rosy. "Will Len wait for us, Sid?"

Len had come round to the back of the lorry to help them out, his cigarette glowing red at the side of his mouth.

Sidney jumped down and spoke to him in a low voice. Len seemed a man of few words.

Then Sidney said, "'E says 'e'll wait for thirty minutes. All right, Tills?"

"It'll have to be," said Tilly, as Len lifted her down.

Once they were all on the road, Rudi pulled a torch out of his pocket and the beam lit up a gravel drive on the other side of the open gate.

"Come on," said Tilly striding forward, trying to look brave.

But if she was honest, she was more terrified than she'd ever been in her life.

It would be easier to face Hitler and his stupid bombs right now, she thought, than walk into this strange house and beg Aunt Edith to save the pets.

Chapter 21

AUNT EDITH

Sunday night, 3rd September 1939

The drive was quite long and they couldn't see the house – especially as there weren't any lights showing. An owl hooted in the trees, but it didn't sound like the friendly owl in their woods by the den. Tilly was shaking with nerves and she wasn't sure if she could even speak – her throat felt closed tight.

Then they rounded a bend and the dark shape of the house appeared, with a great sweep of drive leading up to it.

"We can't go in the front door," whispered Tilly.

"Follow me," said Sid, and he made off to the side of the house, bending low to avoid being spotted.

They all bent down too, and Rudi turned off his torch.

Sidney found an open doorway halfway down and dodged inside. They followed and found themselves in what looked like a boot room.

"Where will they be, do you think?" asked Miles. "It's gone eight."

"Maybe they're having dinner," said Tilly.

Sidney had gone further into the room and now he called out in a loud whisper, "Over 'ere. There's a door."

As they tiptoed forward, Sidney turned the handle and opened it a crack.

They heard the irritated voice of a man call out, "Get a move on, Peters. Mr Highcliffe-Barnes is waiting for the brandy."

"Sorry, Mr Jameson, sir," came the reply.

Tilly froze, holding her breath, as they waited for the footsteps to die away.

Then Sidney slipped through the door and they all followed. Tilly's heart was beating so loudly she expected to be stopped any second and told to keep the noise down.

They found themselves in a huge hall with a red carpeted staircase in the middle, leading up to a gallery. A chandelier was suspended from the ceiling over their heads, the crystals winking like diamonds.

"Cor, look at that," said Sid, in his ordinary voice.

"Shhh!" whispered Rosy. "Which way, Tilly?"

Tilly looked all round the hall. There were a bewildering number of doors on each side, all of them shut. Which one should she choose?

Suddenly, they heard footsteps again, and Sidney whispered, "Come on. Get behind the stairs."

They all rushed around the back of the stairs, huddling down in the shadows.

Then, to Tilly's horror, she heard the irritated man call out, "Oi, you young scallywag. Stop right there!"

Oh no! she thought. They've seen Sid.

But Sidney called out in his cheeky voice, "Am I glad to see you, Mister. I was just passing, like, and I thought I sees a rat run in the back door, so I comes in to check the young ladies of the 'ouse is all right."

"Don't you Mister me. Peters, grab him, we'll see what the police have to say about this."

"Yes sir, Mr Jameson," said the other man.

Tilly was just about to step out of the shadows and stick up for Sidney when a great shout went up, "Look out! Don't let him get away! Don't just stand there, man – go after him."

A heavy, lumbering tread sounded down the hall and faded away.

Miles was laughing silently – so hard that tears were coming into his eyes. "Good old Sid," he spluttered. "They'll never catch him."

"Hush," whispered Tilly. "Someone else might hear us. Sid's bought us some time, but not much."

Just then, she heard another door open, and there was Sophia saying, "Aunt Edith, how long will the drive to Sussex take tomorrow? I'm worried about Horace."

Found her! thought Tilly, almost crying out with excitement and nerves. Rosy gasped beside her and Miles whispered something in Rudi's ear.

A woman answered, with a rather deep but warm voice. "It will take a few hours, so I do hope you're not going to whine in the car, child."

Aunt Edith, thought Tilly. And she doesn't sound quite so stuck up as Sophia's ghastly mother. But can I be sure?

She pulled herself forward and peered round the stairs in time to see a door nearby close. Rosy pulled her back, hissing, "They'll see you. What can we do anyway? The police will arrive in a minute."

But suddenly Tilly didn't care.

We've come all this way and overcome a million obstacles to save our pets, she told herself. Now I have to go in there and ask for help, and I mustn't whine whatever happens. Aunt Edith obviously hates whiny children.

She turned to Rosy and the others. Their eyes were gleaming in the light from the chandelier which flickered round the back of the stairs. They were crouched down, looking up at her, as if they completely trusted that she could solve this final problem.

"Everyone stay here," she whispered. "I'll go by myself. Sid will be fine. He can take care of himself. If anything happens, make your getaway with Len. That way, I'll be the only one to get into trouble, and they'll never know you were here."

There was a silence as they stared at her.

Tilly wasn't sure she could stand upright as her legs were so shaky, let alone walk into the room without falling over.

Then Miles said, "Don't be a nincompoop. We're all coming, aren't we, Cobras?"

"Tilly, you're so *silly* sometimes."

"*Ja, doof tep.*"

"But... I... I... don't think..." stammered Tilly.

"Lead on," said Rosy, in her Megan voice.

Tilly stared at her for a few seconds, then she stood up, throwing her shoulders back, and said, "All right, let's get it over with."

They followed as she marched up to the door, turned the handle and pushed it open.

They found themselves in a brightly lit room with a good fire burning in the grate. The room was quite large and there were sofas and armchairs grouped around the fire. Two women in smart black dresses sat smoking on the sofas. Tilly recognized one of the women as Sophia's mother. Was the other one Aunt Edith? She'd only seen her from the back on the High Street.

Sophia was curled up in an armchair with a book. When she saw Tilly and the others, her mouth dropped open.

Before anyone could speak, Tilly said, "Please... could I... would it be possible—"

But Sophia cut her off. "Hello," she said. "Mummy, you remember the children from the woods."

Tilly wasn't sure if Sophia was on their side or about to give them away, but Miles seemed very certain.

"You traitor!" he cried.

"After everything we've done for your Horace," said Rosy, sticking her chin in the air. Dorothy mewed and gave a miniature snort.

Sophia's mother was getting up and reaching for what looked like a bell.

Tilly's heart dropped to the floor. Now we'll be arrested, she thought.

Then she caught a look of interest on the other woman's face as she stared at them, her head tipped to one side, eyebrows raised as if to say, I'm listening.

That must be Aunt Edith, Tilly thought, and suddenly all the strength and courage she needed rushed up through her.

"Please listen." She looked directly at the woman who stared back at her with a steady gaze. "I think you're Aunt Edith – who cares enough about an old goat with arthritis to save him from the bombs – and we've come here today to ask you if you could find room for *our* pets too. I know they're only ordinary London pets and we are…" she looked round at the others, "well, we're just ordinary London children, and we can't pay you or anything, but we'd be eternally grateful if you could save our pets from Hitler's bombs."

"For goodness' sakes, Edith," said Sophia's mother, "I'm going to ring for Jameson and get these… these—"

"—unusual children, I think are the words you're looking for, Marjorie," Aunt Edith said, in an imposing, deep voice.

Phew, thought Tilly. It is her. But is she on our side?

Sophia's mother stopped in her tracks, a puzzled frown on her face.

"I quite agree, they're very unusual," went on Aunt Edith.

Her gaze swept across the rather muddy group of Cobras, coming to rest on Tilly's hot red face. Sophia had put her book down and stood up, her eyebrows furrowed with worry. Would she stick up for them or throw them to the lions?

"We're not really unusual, just pet lov—" began Tilly, but she was cut off by a huge commotion in the hall and the thudding of feet.

A man's voice shouted, "Grab him!"

Sidney burst into the room, rolled across the carpet and ended up on his knees.

"Smashing 'ere, ain't it, Tills?" he called out, as two men ran into the room and grabbed him.

"Let me go. I ain't done nothing!" yelled Sidney, struggling as the men fought to pin his arms by his side.

"Put him down!" called out Aunt Edith in her imperious voice. "He's with these children, I expect."

She raised her eyebrows at Tilly who nodded back.

"Edith, I very much—" started Sophia's mother, with a furious look on her face.

"Not now, Marjorie," said Aunt Edith, looking down her nose at the other woman.

Sophia's mother sat down and, picking up a fan from the table, began to fan herself violently.

The two men, their faces all hot and sweaty, let Sidney go.

He brushed his ragged clothes down as though they were the finest tailored suit and said, "Thank you, me old son." Then he turned to Aunt Edith and said, "Blimey missus, you got a lotta books in that room opposite. I nearly 'ad time to read off all the names by Mr Dickens."

Aunt Edith's eyebrows shot so far up her face, Tilly thought they'd fly into the air.

"Do you read a lot, young man?"

"Me teacher, Miss Cotton, lends me books. I'm 'alfway through *David Copperfield*. They sent 'im to a right 'orrible school, ain't they?"

Aunt Edith stared at him for a minute and then she said to Tilly, "I thought you said you *weren't* unusual children."

She looked around the room and, catching Sophia's eye, she said, "So have you been playing nicely, Sophia, with such lovely friends?"

"I should very much hope not, my girl!" cried out her mother in horror.

But to Tilly's surprise, Sophia stuck her chin in the air and said in a rather wobbly voice, "Tilly and her friends saved Horace's life – and so they saved my life. Please help them, Aunt Edith – I'm afraid mummy doesn't understand."

"How dare—" began Sophia's mother.

But Aunt Edith cut her off: "Sophia, pass the chocolates like a good hostess—"

"You'll do no such thing!" spluttered Sophia's mother.

"I rather think Sophia will be wise to pass the chocolates like a good hostess if we're going to have a pleasant war together in *my* country home, Marjorie." Then she flicked her cigarette ash into a glass ashtray on the coffee table, where there was a huge box of chocolates.

There was a deep silence, during which Sophia's mother suddenly needed to fan herself again very hard and Sophia went brick red.

Then Aunt Edith said, "Sophia?"

Sophia shot a frightened glance at her mother, and then she picked up the box and passed it round the children. They took one chocolate each, but Tilly noticed that Sidney managed to get several more up his sleeve.

"Now then," said Aunt Edith. "I can't think why you haven't told us you've been playing with such a lovely group of children over the summer, Sophia. Come closer, child," she beckoned to Tilly. "Tell me all about it – and what are your names?"

So Tilly told her all about the emergency zoo, why they had hidden their pets and about Alec breaking his leg. She even explained about Rudi, and that he wasn't the enemy. Rudi gave a polite bow when Tilly said his name, and Aunt Edith gave an approving nod.

"...and so you see, please, you are our absolute last hope. Most of us are being evacuated in the morning..." Tilly glanced round at Rosy who gave her a shrug, her little cat mewing in her arms. "We can't let our pets starve to death."

"Absolutely not," said Aunt Edith. "Marjorie," she turned to the other woman. "I've said it before and I'll say it again, your Sophia needs to mix more widely – otherwise how on earth can she possibly learn about friendship and loyalty? We all have to pull together if we are going to defeat Mr Hitler. Now, these children," her hand swept imperiously across The Cobras, "they already have the right qualities to go to war and win."

"Well, to be quite frank, Edith, I've been worried for some time about Sophia—"

"Mummy!" cried out Sophia. "How could you! You know that I've begged you to let me go and play with local children like Tilly and Rosy and you're such a… well… a snob. Well, I'm not, and these children are my best friends, so there!"

She met Tilly's eyes, who gave her a firm nod, and the older girl managed a small smile. Sidney gave a loud snort and Miles grinned at Rudi, who muttered something in German under his breath.

"Well said, Sophia. Time you listened to your daughter, Marjorie," said Aunt Edith and then, turning back to The

Cobras, she went on, "I'll take all the pets. Have them ready by seven o'clock tomorrow morning. I'll send my driver with a van to take them down to Sussex. Sophia will ride in the van to make sure they are all safe..." She raised an eyebrow at Sophia who gave a firm nod.

"I've been a member of the Dumb Animals League since I was your age, Sophia," said Aunt Edith, "and we plan to rescue as many pets as possible from all this senseless slaughter and give them safe homes in the countryside. And, for your information, Marjorie, not just the pets of rich people."

She smiled in such a kind fashion towards the children that Tilly knew she could trust her completely. "We thank you from the bottom of our hearts," she said. "Only—" Her nerve failed her.

"Come on, child," said Aunt Edith. "Speak up."

"Could we please write and ask how our pets are doing?"

"Of course – what a clever idea. You're obviously very well educated." Aunt Edith threw a contemptuous glance at Sophia's mother. Then she opened a huge black handbag on the sofa beside her and pulled out some cards. "Take one each. You have my address and telephone number. Contact me if you need anything."

Her gaze lingered for a moment on Sidney's thin face. He lowered his eyes and shoved his hands in his pockets.

Then Rosy said, "Gosh! Look at the time. We have to go – Len won't wait for us and we'll never get home!"

Chapter 22

WHEREVER WE END UP

Sunday night to Tuesday morning, 5th September 1939

After saying their thankyous and goodbyes, The Cobras raced out of the house and down the drive, laughing and whooping to each other.

"Sophia was so brave standing up to her mum," said Tilly.

"Agreed," said Rosy. "Did you see the look on her mum's face when Sidney swiped all those chocolates?"

"I was just rescuing 'em for my mum."

"Three cheers for Tilly," cried Rosy. "She's saved the emergency zoo."

They cheered and shouted *Doof tep* all the way to the lorry.

As they bounced back down the dark roads, for the first time Tilly thought about Mum and Dad and how worried they must be – sitting at home, watching the clock and wondering if she'd got lost in the blackout. It was after nine, and neither she nor Rosy, and probably Miles and Rudi too, had ever been out so late. She couldn't vouch for Sidney, as the Scudders seemed to practically bring themselves up.

Len let them out at Sidney's flats and Miles disappeared off home. Rosy, Rudi and Tilly walked off together towards their streets. Suddenly, a group of adults appeared, and a great stream of German poured across the street. It was Lotte shrieking at the top of her voice. Mum, Dad, Megan and Donald were hurrying along behind her.

Racing up, Lotte grabbed Rudi and hugged him so tight Tilly thought she'd crush him to death.

Then Megan reached Rosy and, with tears pouring down her cheeks, she cried out, "My darling little sister." She enveloped Rosy in a bear hug, sobbing, "I was terrified something awful had happened to you. I promised Mum on her deathbed that I'd look after you."

Donald was patting Megan's arm and Rosy was sobbing too.

Before Tilly could say anything, Mum grabbed her, folding her arms around her and whispered, "I was so scared I'd lost you too."

Tilly couldn't help sniffing into Mum's raincoat then, and Mum stifled a sob.

Then Dad said, "Come on, time to go home. The kiddies are safe."

Everyone muttered their agreement and, calling to Lotte and Rudi to walk with them, they set off arm in arm.

As they walked through the dark, eerie streets, Dad looked up at the night sky and said, "Whatever happens in this war, you can't black out the stars."

"You're right there, Wilf," agreed Donald.

They went to Rudi's foster parents first and left him together with Lotte, who was invited to stay the night.

"See you both in the morning," Tilly managed to whisper before they parted. "Seven sharp. We'll save Hanno – you'll see."

Rosy, Donald and Megan called their goodbyes at the next corner and then Tilly was home – without her darling Bonny, but with Mum and Dad, tucked up in her own little bed after cheese on toast and a hot bath.

She fell asleep and awoke to hear the cheep, cheep, chirrup of a sparrow singing outside her window. Grabbing her watch, she could see it was six thirty. Dad was in the bathroom, whistling as he shaved. Mum was downstairs, clearing out the grate in the kitchen boiler, rattling the metal cinders tray back and forth.

Tilly leapt out of bed, pulled on her clothes, sneaked downstairs and out of the front door, holding her breath. Good practice for the bombing, she told herself as she grabbed her bike and set off for the canal.

Rosy was waiting for her on the bridge.

"I'm coming with you," said Rosy, when Tilly pedalled up.

"Where?" said Tilly, bewildered. Are we running away now? she wondered. I haven't packed anything.

"Evacuation. I can take Dorothy, too. Megan was so upset last night because she thought I'd run away, she gave in."

"Crikey!" breathed Tilly.

"Come on," said Rosy, "we don't want to miss the van."

They rode off between the factories and across the fields, the morning sun already warm on their backs. The other Cobras were already at the hut – except Mary, who wasn't allowed out any more, Conor, who was probably halfway to Scotland with Boxer, and Alec, who couldn't walk.

Lotte was with Rudi, who had Hanno in his arms and the bugle over his shoulder. They were whispering to each other in German and Rudi was nodding.

The Scudders had bags on their backs.

"We kissed mummy goodbye," said Pam, in tears. "Neville's taking us to be 'vacuated."

"We ain't got no one to wave us off," said Sidney.

Neville told him to shut up.

But Tilly's heart went out to the Scudders – probably hungry, with no new clothes for their great adventure.

"Rosy and I'll come and wave you off," said Tilly.

"Course," said Rosy.

Pam and Sidney cheered, and even Neville looked pleased.

Then a man broke through into the clearing with Sophia, who called out, "The van's here."

With solemn looks and many tears, the children brought their pets to the open doors of the van, Sophia carrying the guinea pigs.

Tilly carried Bonny in her arms, whispering in her floppy ear how much she loved her. Tears poured down her face and Bonny was licking them away, but Tilly knew she had to give her up to save her life.

"We'll be together again, I promise, my darling Bonny Bonbons," she whispered.

Tilly handed Bonny up to the man who settled her in a basket in the corner, tying her to a hook on the wall. Bonny started to whine straight away, pulling on her lead, her paws scrabbling on the wicker basket.

"Aunt Edith says we have to be there before lunch, so we need to leave now," said Sophia. "I'm so sorry, but I promise we will take very good care of all the pets." She put a hand out and patted Tilly on the arm.

Tilly gave her a nod and, wiping her wet cheeks, she said in a hoarse voice, "We'll always be The Cobras – whatever happens."

Sidney piped up, "Three cheers for Tilly and the emergency zoo!"

The Cobras, including Sophia, who looked round at them with pride on her face, cheered.

Tilly turned back to Bonny – she had slumped down, her snub spaniel nose resting on the edge of the basket, liquid brown eyes staring mournfully at Tilly as if to say, *Don't send me away, please.*

She nearly jumped into the van to set the little dog free, but the driver came round from the cab and slammed the doors shut. Sophia gave a wave and, calling her goodbyes, climbed into the front next to the driver's seat.

"Goodbye, my darling Bonny Bonbons, goodbye, goodbye," called out Tilly, over and over, tears pouring down her cheeks as the van pulled away. "Don't forget me."

She broke into great, heaving sobs, and Rosy put her arm around her waist and laid her head on her friend's shoulder.

They stood there until the van had bumped over the fields and out of sight, heading back to the road.

Neville said, "We'd better go."

The Scudders picked up their bags and Tilly's sobs calmed down to a hiccup. Rosy helped her pick up her bike.

The Cobras rode for the last time over the fields and back to the canal as larks soared above the corn and into the brilliant blue sky. They counted four barrage balloons above the rooftops of their streets – there was no pretending any more that the German bombers weren't coming.

But Rosy and I will be together, Tilly reminded herself – and at least I know Bonny is safe, although she felt unbearably sad. I'm glad I'm going away as well. Bonny and I will be homesick together.

They first went to the Scudders's flats and left the bikes in the yard. Then they walked round to Canal Street School where the children joined their different classes. A teacher blew three loud blasts on her whistle and the long crocodile set off.

"Goodbye Neville, goodbye Sidney, goodbye Pam!" called out Tilly, and Sidney turned and gave them his cheeky grin.

"Good luck!" cried Rosy, and then they were gone.

Miles had disappeared before they reached the flats, but Lotte and Rudi had come with them to see the Scudders off.

"We want to say thank you," said Lotte, holding Rudi's hand. They were both staring with their wide, brown eyes at Tilly. "You have been such good friend, and please to keep eye on Rudi when he goes on your bus tomorrow."

Tilly nodded and they all walked off.

CHAPTER 22

Tilly spent the rest of the day helping Mum and packing her things – stopping often to wipe a tear away when she thought about Bonny.

Then it was Tuesday morning. She was sitting on the bus with Rosy and Dorothy; Rudi was in the seat in front of them. Mum had thrust a huge packet of sandwiches into Tilly's hands at the last minute, tears pouring down her face. Tilly was already gripped with homesickness. When would she see her parents again? What if they got bombed? But she didn't want to upset Mum even more, so she forced a grin and called out "goodbye" and "write soon".

The bus took off and they all waved madly out of the window. Within minutes, their families, their school and the London streets they had grown up in and knew like the backs of their hands were gone. When would they see them again?

Rosy linked her hand in Tilly's and they settled Dorothy between them. Tilly could feel the kitten's little body rise and fall with her steady breathing.

"I wonder where we're going," said Rosy, as they stared out of the window.

"Wherever we end up, I'm going to write to Aunt Edith every week and ask how Bonny is," declared Tilly.

Rosy nodded as Tilly felt in her pocket for Aunt Edith's address card.

Bonny will always be *my* dog, no matter how long this war lasts, was Tilly's final thought before she fell asleep to the sound of wheels rolling along the country roads.

Author's Note

As the outbreak of World War II approached, people started to destroy their pets, as they believed they would not cope with bombs and gas, and couldn't be fed when rationing came in. It is estimated that around 750,000 pets, mainly cats and dogs, were destroyed in Britain.

Organizations such as the Dumb Animal League did their best to save as many pets as possible, but they could not halt the initial slaughter. However, at the end of the week after war was declared, the population came to their senses and, with great remorse, published letters in the newspapers, apologizing to their deceased pets.

When I read this largely unknown story of World War II in a short newspaper article, my first thought was, What would the children do? There must have been many children like Tilly and Rosy who felt desperate to save their pets – and so my story was born.

For the writing of this book, I am grateful for comments from Savita and Hish Kalhan who kindly read a draft, as well as to Leslie Wilson who also read a draft and advised me on the German.

Margaret Mackay, Librarian at the Highgate Scientific and Literary Institute, helped find suitable books for research. Bridget Harrison, writer and biographer, shared her memories of a childhood before the war. In addition, I read diaries from the Mass Observation archives at the British Library for details of each day in the week leading up to the declaration of war.

Many thanks to Anne Kirk, who came on the Kindertransport from Germany in April 1939, for allowing me to read the correspondence between herself and her mother and quote from it. Her husband, Bob, also a Kindertransport child, translated the letters from German for me and gave background information. Sadly their parents and most of their family perished in the Holocaust.

To my publishers, Elisabetta Minervini and Alessandro Gallenzi, and to all at Alma – especially Will Dady – many thanks for bringing this book to publication. Bella Pearson's editorial input was absolutely invaluable. A heartfelt thanks to my agent, Anne Clark, for her perseverance and belief in my writing. The loyal support of my husband, Rafael Halahmy, continues to underpin my work and life.

AUTHOR'S NOTE

Writing this book has allowed me to revisit my own childhood in the 1960s – when children roamed free and only returned home when it was dark. I hope this book shows how much fun we had.

– Miriam Halahmy

London, 2016